Talking About
Growing Up

♡ you, Caroline

Maryjane
Caselli

You are a star ♡

A Girl's World Presents

Talking About
GROWING UP

Real-Life
Advice from
Girls Like You

Created by A Girl's World Productions, Inc.
www.agirlsworld.com

Edited by J. Christine Gardner
With Lynn Barker and Karen Willson

PRIMA GIRLS
An Imprint of Prima Publishing
3000 Lava Ridge Court • Roseville, California 95661
(800) 632-8676 • www.primalifestyles.com

Library of Congress Cataloging-in-Publication Data
Talking about growing up / A Girl's World Productions Inc.
    p. cm. — (Prima Girls series)
    ISBN 0-7615-3291-9
    1. Teenage girls—Psychology—Juvenile literature. 2. Teenage girls—Social conditions—Juvenile literature. 3. Preteens—Psychology—Juvenile literature. 4. Preteens—Social conditions—Juvenile literature. I Girl's World Productions, Inc. II. Series

HQ798.T353 2001
305.235—dc21   2001021412

01 02 03 04 HH 10 9 8 7 6 5 4 3 2 1

Printed in the United States of America

How to Order
Single copies may be ordered from Prima Publishing, 3000 Lava Ridge Court, Roseville, CA 95661; telephone (800) 632-8676 ext. 4444. Quantity discounts are also available. On your letterhead, include infor-mation concerning the intended use of the books and the number of books you wish to purchase.

Visit us online at www.primalifestyles.com

First, with grateful hearts we dedicate this book to God, who in 1996 gave us the idea to go out and build a place on the Internet where what girls think, feel, and do really does matter.

We dedicate this book to the millions of girls who have used their time and talent to share their thoughts, hopes, and dreams with all the other girls of the world at www.agirlsworld.com.

With love and peace, we dedicate this book to all our volunteer girl editors (past and present), our AGW Girlcrew, our adult volunteers, advisers, webmaster, family, and friends who made A Girl's World a reality.

Contents

Preface

Hello, I'm Juanita Christine Gardner and I'm a member of the girlcrew that runs www.agirlsworld.com, A Girl's World Online Clubhouse. Since 1996, our free online magazine has been publishing real-life advice and daily, weekly, and monthly features written and edited for girls by girls and teens the world over. Girls around the world use the Web to come to AGW and submit advice questions to be answered. Our volunteer advice columnists write an answer and send it back to the club to be published weekly. If you have the Web, here's where you can find advice: http://www.agirlsworld.com /info/advice.html.

But not every girl has the Internet. So that's where we got the idea to publish this book. We want every girl to get advice from real girls and teens like you!

This book is for girls who have all kinds of questions and need answers, but maybe they are too embarrassed to ask their mom, or maybe they don't have a mom. I'm editing this book because I can relate to things that are tough. Being a girl is very hard in our world today. Girls face problems, like wondering, "Am I ugly?" or "Do I have more pimples than she does?" and other things like that. I want this book to make girls around the world feel that they're not alone with their problems.

I was very pleased to edit this book. It told me a lot of things that either I've wondered about or didn't even think about. I think girls reading this book will gain a lot of confidence, but this book has a lot more than just advice. There are cool quotes; poems; Talk Abouts; journal ideas and places to doodle; and WEBwatch, ideas for things you and your friends can do together to find answers to your problems.

If you have any questions or comments about this book, you can e-mail me on www.agirlsworld.com. I'd love to hear from you! My penpal number is 199221.

Sincerely,

Juanita Christine Gardner
Girl Editor, A Girl's World Online Clubhouse

About A Girl's World: What Makes This Book Special

"Help me! I'm desperate!" Whether it's dealing with a first crush, family or financial crisis, or peer pressure, pre-teen and teen girls most appreciate advice from their peers. Getting real-life advice for girls, by girls is what this book is all about.

The "Tuff Talk" area on A Girl's World is where questioning girls can ask their peers to help them with more serious issues. Since some of our girls are as young as age 7 and our site is family-oriented and approved by several educational associations, we don't tackle issues of "the first time," or pregnancy, rape, abortion, and so on. But if a girl is worried about buying her first bra, we're there to help.

So, is the situation at home or school totally stressing you out? Friends or 'rents or teachers scaring you? Need advice on how to deal? Don't bug out! Read on! This is the space where girls get to "dish" about all the troubles they have growing up. In the pre-teen and teen years, emotions are fluctuating and what might seem a tiny ripple in the tranquility pool to adults is a mighty tsunami (huge wave!) to many girls. Issues of betrayal, abandonment, family separation, moving away, being popular, whatever life throws at a girl—however embarrassing or challenging—another girl has been through it and can help.

The material in this book was written, edited, and suggested by girls and teens. Girls ask the questions and their peers, not grownups, answer them. As members of the adult "Girl's World" team, we had the opportunity to collect, shape, and do a final edit on this book. But what you're holding is truly girl-powered, and that's what makes it special. It was important to our Girlcrew that readers are able to react to what they read here. That's why we hope you enjoy the many opportunities to journal, doodle, talk to your friends, and turn this book into a one-of-a-kind treasure chest you've created that will reflect the experiences of the most important girl in the world—YOU!

Lynn Barker and Karen Willson
Adult Editors, A Girl's World Online Clubhouse

Introduction

Share the Dream

Everything in this book and on our Web site was thought up, planned out, written, and edited by girls and teens the world over. Our mission is to create a space in the world that is entirely girl-powered. We're all about what's possible in a bright future created entirely for and by girls and teens.

After you've read this book, you're invited to get in on the fun. Do you have any stories or advice you'd like to contribute? Your thoughts and opinions about this book really matter to us. Here's how to get in touch or send us submissions for the next book on how to deal with tough problems.

Submissions online:
http://www.agirlsworld.com/clubgirl/scoop/index.html

Comments online:
http://www.agirlsworld.com/problems.html

Submissions or comments by e-mail:
editor@agirlsworld.com

Subject line:
Talk About: Growing Up Book

Mailing Address:
A Girl's World Productions, Inc.
ATTN: Talking About Books Editor
825 College Blvd.
PBO 102-442
Oceanside, CA 92057
(760) 414-1092 messages

1

The Me Nobody Knows

First: Who Am I?

Everyone great and small has problems. The first step in solving problems is getting to know your greatest resource: yourself. That means getting to know everything about who you are. The next few pages should help you get started. Fill in as many blanks as you can. Leave anything blank that doesn't apply to you. There are cool places to go to find out some of the answers. Have fun finding out things you don't know!

Journalize It!

MY LIFE!
(A Quick Autobiography of Me)

(Either paste or draw a picture of yourself in the frame, then decorate the cool frame with GELLYZ pens or your fav marker!)

Here's a picture of ME!

Hi! My name is _____.

But I like my friends to call me (nickname)
_____.

Want to know where I got my nickname? Here's what happened:

My favorite exclamation is _____
(like Cool!, Radical!, Far Out!, or whatever)

Journalize It!

I am _____ years old.

I was born on (date) _____, which is on this day of the week: _____. (To find out WHICH DAY, go here: http://www.agirlsworld.com /games/jscript/birth-day/birth-day.html)

I was born in (state/country)

_____.

Here's a fun piece of trivia about the state where I was born (To find out WHAT cool U.S. trivia happened in your state, go here: http://www.netstate.com/states/)

Get this! This famous thing happened the same day I was born: (To find out WHAT, go to the "History Channel's This Day in History" at this Web site: http://www .historychannel.com/today/)

Did you know? Here's a famous woman who shares my birthday: _____. (To find out WHO, go to the "Women's International Birthday Calendar" at this site: http://www.wic.org /cal/idex_cal.htm)

She's famous because _____

_____.

(continues)

Journalize It!

Here's a picture of my house:

More important, here's my room:

This is what I think about my room. It's totally (description) _____

_____.

Except for the (name it!) _____,
of course.

If I had my choice, I'd add this to my room (something you want): _____

That's because I really want to (what? why?) _____

_____

Journalize It!

If I were a country with a flag, it would look like this:

My proudest moment: The thing I've done so far in my life that I'm the most proud of is this:

Here's a picture of ME doing something cool!

Roles

You sit next to them in class every day. The Whiz Kid. The Teacher's Pet. The Prom Queen. Mr. Cool. Miss Jock. The Complainer. The Psycho. The Dreamer. Miss Happy. Mr. Sad Sack. The Drama-rama. The Slacker. Miss Perfect. The Leech. The Animal. The Brain. The Preppie. The Class Clown. Everyone falls into roles.

What role do you play at school? I'm the

_____.

What do you like about it?

nothing

What do you hate about it?

everything

Do you think it's fair that people see you this way?

yes

Draw a picture of a NEW role you'd like to play at school.

[ ]

Now name that role: _____

Think about ways you could try that role out and write them down here. You go, girl!

Not So Innocent

There used to be a blank sheet here.
So cold and untamed,
Beckoning me.
Its power was astonishing;
Red and blue lines that could
    hold so much,
taunt so much,
and not even be noticed.
It broke my will;
I gave in.
I was never trying to resist it,
but it still sucked me in.
Its force was overpowering.
I am heard this way
and no other.
Without the encouragement
of a blank sheet,
nothing would be as it is.
Nothing would be heard, known, seen.
All novels were once blank;
All constitutions, all contracts
were once blank sheets,
coaxing inner anguish to spill out
in a few strikes of black lead;
Coaxing the brain to show fear, hatred,
and change.
The innocent blank sheet
is not so innocent.
It is the man's will to sign or not sign,
but it is the paper that has the dotted line.
Many sheets tell stories,
but all have stories to tell.
They are not so innocent now.

—Written by Ashley, 13, Maryland

Life is what we make it, always has been, always will be.
—Grandma Moses
Submitted by
Zindy-Ann, 15, Texas

Honors Class Is Too Tuff!

"You Can Quote Me on That"

Honesty and frankness will make you vulnerable. Be honest and frank anyway.

—Mother Teresa

Submitted by

Laura, 13, Alabama

The Problem I have gotten a lot of bad grades on my report card. According to my mom, it is because of my organizational skills. I don't think that's the only reason. I am in an honors class and things are really tuff. I really want to go to a regular class. I told my mom and she talked to the principal, and he doesn't want me to leave the honors class. What should I do?

— Liz, 10, Indiana

A Solution   Hey Liz! Well, if the principal doesn't want you to leave the honors class, then that might mean that he thinks you can do much better than what you have been doing. He has confidence in you. I am in high school, and I took some classes that I didn't think I could get through once I was in there. Now I am doing much better and am about to go into higher classes for next year. At first I didn't want to go through with some of my classes, but my parents told me to stick in there, and by the end of the semester, if I still didn't like them, then I could switch. I agreed to that and by the end of the semester, I didn't want to change because I got the hang of it.

You will do the same thing. Just stick in there for a while and study as much as you can to do well in your classes. If by the end you still don't want to go on with your honors classes, then talk to your mom and then talk to your principal yourself and explain your problems. But before you decide to switch, go to Study Buddy at http://www.studybuddy.com. That should help you with some of your organizing and other study problems.

Good Luck!

—Casey, 14, Tennessee

Imaginations

Imagine
Only a single tree in the park
OR Only a single cherry
*   blossom*
that blooms during its season

Imagine
A lone crane without a mate
OR a Man without
*   companions*

Imagine
Sun existing without Moon
OR Night existing without
*   Day*

Imagine
Life without Life
OR Emotion . . . without
Happiness, Ecstasy, Peace or Love

One shall hope these are merely
Imaginations.

You Can Quote Me on That

People don't always have the vision. The secret for the person with the vision is to stand up. It takes a lot of courage.
—Natalie Cole
Submitted by
Natalia, 15, USA

—Written by Edlyn, 11, Singapore
Edited by Melody, 13, California

My Temper Is Too Hot to Handle!

The Problem I'm an average girl with enough friends and companions, but sometimes my temper heats up and I can't stop it. My attitude is bad and I'm not afraid to admit it, but I want to change BADLY! Please, if anyone has advice on how I can stop getting so mad so often, tell me!

—Alyssa, 11

A Solution Hey Alyssa! You are not the only person with a temper problem. My dad and I, we can really lose it. I didn't realize how bad my temper was until one of my best friends told me that I overreact to little things. That made me really mad, but as soon as I opened my mouth to snarl at her, I didn't have anything to say. I realized she was right. So here is what I did. First, when I got angry, before I would say anything, I would try to see it from another point of view. Is this really worth yelling about? Is it something that will pass, or can I live with it? Does it really matter?

If it was no big deal or there was nothing I could do about it, I would go to my room and punch a pillow—hard. You know how sometimes you can get so angry that you just want to scream? Well, do it. Scream, yell, cry, just get it all out. But just don't yell *at* someone. That would be defeating the purpose. And you feel ten times better, just letting it out.

"You Can Quote Me on That"

I do, because I must do something.

—Mother Teresa
Submitted by
Kayleigh, 13, USA

Then came the hard part. I had to swallow my pride and talk to my friends. I told them I get angry over little things and I need their help to change. They were really helpful. Anytime they saw I was about to bite someone's head off, they would tell me to back off and count to ten. You have to think about what you are going to say—before you say it. It helps. If you have to think before you yell, you tend to be nicer with what you say. And it calms you down. I hope these tips help you. Stay cool!

— Lindsay, 14, Louisiana

The Rain Princess

I stare out of my window
Into the pouring rain.
I see a little girl there
Dancing free of pain.

I can hear her little giggles
Out there in the night.
I see her body dancing 'round
Out in the pale moonlight.

I feel a grin come to my lips
As she crawls inside.
If her mother knew what she
*   had done*
She'd surely skin her hide.

Without a grunt, without a noise
Without a single sound,
She lifts herself up to my window
Smiling a smile so proud.

ANGER MANAGEMENT

How do you keep your cool when you're mad? Kids' Health has a terrific article on what to do when you're angry, and anger busters.

Check it out right here:

http://www.kidshealth.org/kid/feeling/anger.html

Q. My older brother hits me sometimes. What would you do if it was your brother?

—Anonymous, USA

There's no right or wrong answer. Just circle what you think. Then look over your answers and talk about them with your friends.

1 I'd tell my parents and leave it to them to discipline him.

Mostly disagree   Somewhat disagree   Somewhat agree   Mostly agree

2 I'd talk to a school or church counselor.

Mostly disagree   Somewhat disagree   Somewhat agree   Mostly agree

3 I'd confront him and tell him I'll start hitting back if he doesn't stop.

Mostly disagree   Somewhat disagree   Somewhat agree   Mostly agree

4 I'd hit him back the next time he does it.

Mostly disagree   Somewhat disagree   Somewhat agree   Mostly agree

5 I'd look into anger management activities (like boxing, aerobic training, martial arts, etc.) and try to get my brother interested.

Mostly disagree   Somewhat disagree   Somewhat agree   Mostly agree

Her little limber body
Moves quickly to the bed.
I wonder what she's thinking,
What's going through her
    head?

Does she even realize
That her clothes are dripping
    wet?
She'll be even more sick
    tomorrow.
She doesn't care, I bet.

I love this little girl,
This I must confess.
For all the women in my life,
She is my rain princess.

—Written by Brandi, 16,
    South Carolina
Edited by Serene, 15,
    Singapore

*Like success, growing up
doesn't happen overnight.
You will face failures, re-
jections, and difficult
times along the way. But
if you're honest, express
yourself, and hold onto
your self-respect, you'll
definitely be on the right
track. Peace out!*

—Queen Latifah
Submitted by
Michelle, 15, New Jersey

Someone I Look Up To

*I've had a lot of influential people in my life, but besides my mother,
the brightest star is my big sister. Her name is Summer. She married a
man named Andrew. Andrew works with computer technology and
he's a very smart and very nice guy. Summer is studying to become a
reverend, then they want to preach in their own church.*

*Over the years, whenever I was in trouble, Summer defended me.
Whenever my parents would argue, she would take me into another
room and play games with me so that I wouldn't have to hear it. We
write to each other all the time, and we play a game between each
other frequently, where we spell out words to each other instead of*

talking. We do it so fast that it gets on our mom's nerves. We both love to sing and dance, and we've written quite a few songs over the past few months; they are rather goofy, but very true. If you were to compare our lives, they would be tremendously different, but also the same.

These are just some of the reasons that Summer is the brightest star in my life. Even if she wasn't, we'd still love each other just the same, and thank God for that.

—Alyssa, 12, Texas

My Friends Want to Change My Religion!

The Problem My friends keep "witnessing" their religion to me and I'm tired of it. How do I tell them that I don't want to be witnessed to? They can't recruit me. I am the religion I want to be and yet they don't understand. How do I tell them?

—Tiffany, 14, Utah

" You Can Quote Me on That "

We don't see things as they are. We see them as we are.
—Anaïs Nin, Writer
Submitted by
Amber, 12, Georgia

A Solution Dear Tiffany: I think what you should do is, first of all, tell your friends how you feel. Then, if this does not work, also tell your friends that you like your religion and that they should accept you the way you are. One of the ways that can make you "you" is your religion. Tell your friends that they should be happy to be your friend the way you are. This is how friends should act toward one another.

I think that religious beliefs can make you feel good and also happy about yourself. Friends should make you feel the same way and make your self-esteem higher. Your friends are obviously happy in their religion since they are witnessing it to others. You should also say to them that they should not keep people from making their own decisions on important issues, such as religion.

Picking a religion can be a big step in a person's life, and your friends should let people think about this big step. When someone says that they do not want to be a certain religion, they should accept this, let it be, and not keep harping on someone till they give in.

—Jen, 13, Washington

Girls must be encouraged to make a life plan . . . she must learn to compete, not as a woman, but as a human being.
—Betty Naomi Friedan
Submitted by
Brandy, 12, Missouri

When one is a stranger to oneself, then one is estranged from others too.
—Anne Morrow Lindbergh
Submitted by
Melanie, 13, USA

I Am Who I Am

I will never be the popular girl
To whom everyone knows my name.
Nor could I be the weirdest girl
Who stands out just the same.
You try to make me act this way,
Like I'm a puppet for you to play.
I am not like you, but you want me to be.
I can not lie what my feelings are telling me.
And so after days and days, and hours and hours,
My true self begins to flower.
I believe in myself,
And I open my feelings stored on those shelves.
I found my calling and will keep it true;
I am who I am, but I am not you.

—Written by Stephanie

Someone I Look Up To

My dad and my mom both taught me to believe in myself. I learned
that they would be on my side, no matter what I did. I could get in
deep trouble at school, and they would be there to help me. If I got
after-school detention, they would be there to help me get out of it.
(I haven't got any detentions yet, but you get the point!) They
also told me to believe in myself no matter what, and love myself—
even if I think I am fat, too skinny, too ugly, too beautiful, etc.
Whatever people think of me, I don't really care. Whatever I believe
I am, that's what I am. If people think I am fat, or skinny, or
whatever, I don't care. It's all about what I believe I am. My
parents believe in that, too.

—Traci, 11, Iowa

Q. What do you really think of yourself?

— Marie, 14, Canada

There's no right or wrong answer. Just circle what you think. Then look over your answers and talk about them with your friends.

1 I hate myself because I'm not attractive.

Mostly disagree   Somewhat disagree   Somewhat agree   Mostly agree

2 I like who I am and wouldn't change a thing.

Mostly disagree   Somewhat disagree   Somewhat agree   Mostly agree

3 I don't like myself at all! I'm a loser and have no friends.

Mostly disagree   Somewhat disagree   Somewhat agree   Mostly agree

4 I don't think I'll ever get a date.

Mostly disagree   Somewhat disagree   Somewhat agree   Mostly agree

5 I think that I'm a responsible young woman who really respects myself and others.

Mostly disagree   Somewhat disagree   Somewhat agree   Mostly agree

My Boyfriend Dumped Me Because I'm Not Pretty Enough.

The Problem I have a boyfriend. He's really cute. But he says that I look like a tomato. I said to him if he was going to act that way, I'd break up with him. He dumped me yesterday. What should I do? I'm so depressed.

—Erica, 15

A Solution Dear Erica: Personally, I don't see why you're sad that you and that loser aren't together anymore. I mean, he said you look like a tomato? That's not the kind of person you want to be in a relationship with! Even if he is cute, he must have some flaws. And besides, looks don't mean everything.

I know that it seems weird you aren't together anymore. If you want to get back together with him, don't even try. A verbally abusive relationship is something you don't have to put up with! Go talk to friends, your parents, a counselor, someone you trust. Tell this person what happened and what you're feeling. It's better to get it out!

Here are some ways to get it out:

"You Can Quote Me on That"

Don't shut yourself up in a bandbox because you are a woman, but understand what is going on, and educate yourself to take part in the world's work, for it all affects you and yours.

—Louisa May Alcott
Submitted by
Clara, 13, Michigan

Write a long letter to your
   ex-boyfriend explaining how hurt you are. Then rip it up!
   Do not send it to him!

Pour your heart out into your diary.

Have "girls only" nights all the time.

Do some things you didn't do while you were with that guy.

Take up something new like Tai Kwan Do and pretend a
   punching bag is him. Then punch/kick the BEEP! out of the
   punching bag.

   Good luck!

—Jean, 11, Massachusetts

2

Alone and Lonely

Kids on My Bus Avoid Me Like the Plague!

The Problem I have great friends, but none of them rides my bus, and I feel really lonely on the bus. Like this morning, I was in a seat alone, and the two girls who usually sit next to me glanced at me and rushed past the seat I was in, as if they thought I was something gross.

Another day, I was sitting in a seat alone, and an older girl almost sat down next to me, but when she saw it was me, she frowned and sat next to one of the grossest boys in school. I feel like no one on my bus likes me . . . what should I do? I'm too shy to talk to them about it, and I can't stand up to them without someone to back me up.

—Krystel, 12, Ohio

A Solution

Hey Krystel! Don't worry about it. You have friends who care about you. Who cares if anybody on the bus likes you? Only your true friends should matter, though it is nice to make new friends. I used to ride the bus all alone myself. I didn't care because it is just a ride to and from school. There is just one thing you should make sure of. Make sure that all of your school supplies or your other belongings are not on the seat next to you like you are saving it for somebody. It looks like you are waiting for another person to come along and sit with you. Just put your things in your lap or on the floor. That was one problem I had. I would put my stuff up on the seat, like the space was already taken.

The girls who rushed past you probably found an open seat where they could sit together and not separately. All of this is probably your imagination making you think no one likes you. But the best thing to do is ignore it. And also, think of it this way. Having a seat to yourself is always wonderful to have. I can't stand to be in a seat all cramped up because someone is sitting with me. And don't be shy. I am, and I can't stand myself for it sometimes.

—Casey, 14, Tennessee

Editor's Note: Another tip: Just be as friendly as possible even if you are shy. If there are other kids waiting at your bus stop, talk to them a little before getting on the bus, and then maybe they'll sit with you to continue or finish the conversation. Same thing before you get on the bus to go home. Worth a try! You may not have this problem, but some kids are avoided because they just smell funny. So watch those personal hygiene habits. Do you smell like a rose or dirty toes?

Why Hate Me?

Life is one big question waiting to be solved.
Some questions are very easy, some extremely hard.
Mine is a challenging one that can go many ways,

*I say the one I've chosen is the
  one I want to stay.
Is there a reason to hate me
  without knowing me,
When all I'm looking for is a
  way to be free?
I may be different and that is
  very true,
But when will the world look
  without fear of something
  new?!*

— Written by Stacy, 16,
  Minnesota

***Throw your dreams into
space like a kite, and you
do not know what it will
bring back, a new life, a
new friend, a new love, a
new country.***

—Anaïs Nin, from
The Diaries of Anaïs Nin
Submitted by
Jessica, 13, Illinois

Someone I Look Up To

*My best friend is my bright
star because she is one of the
kindest and most friendly people I know. She is really, really sweet
and, unlike some people I know, she treats me like a human being and
always seems to understand my thoughts and feelings. Whenever I'm
worried about something, she not only comforts me but also tries to
help me out with my problem. I can talk to her about anything and
know that she'll understand and won't take offense at anything I say
to her.*

*Sometimes, we are even able to read each other's minds because we
are so alike. You would think this would get annoying after a while,
but surprisingly enough, it doesn't because it just makes us laugh. We
even have the same gloves and schoolbag, but we bought them separately and didn't realize they were the same until we walked into
school wearing the same things! There are even a few things we don't
agree on, which makes our conversations all the more interesting.
Thank you for being my bright star, Laura.*

— Lauren, 14, Scotland

Getting Others to Listen to You

Ever feel like no one wants to listen to what you have to say? Does someone interrupt you all the time before you can finish? Use the box to draw a picture of the person in your life who never listens to you or who cuts you off. Use colored pens to express your feelings. Below the box, use the lines to write that person a note. This is a safe place to tell them exactly what you want to say or to finish your thoughts.

The One Who Doesn't Listen to Me

Q. Survival! Imagine that you are on a deserted island with three strangers. The last person to "survive" will get a million dollars. The other three people disappear! You suspect they're in real danger. What would you do?

There's no right or wrong answer. Just circle what you think. Then look over your answers and talk about them with your friends.

1 People disappeared? All the better. Now there's no one else to compete with for the money.

Mostly disagree   Somewhat disagree   Somewhat agree   Mostly agree

2 I'd go right out right away and look for them. No amount of money is worth ignoring someone who might be hurt or dying.

Mostly disagree   Somewhat disagree   Somewhat agree   Mostly agree

3 Being alone is just too scary. I'd stay in one place but light a bonfire and start yelling their names!

Mostly disagree   Somewhat disagree   Somewhat agree   Mostly agree

4 I'd leave a message behind telling them I was looking for them and start tracing their steps from where they were last seen.

Mostly disagree   Somewhat disagree   Somewhat agree   Mostly agree

5 I'd give them 24 hours to return. Then I'd go look for them.

Mostly disagree   Somewhat disagree   Somewhat agree   Mostly agree

Journalize It!

Too Little Time?

Ever hear yourself say, "I don't have time to learn _____. I'm too busy with _____ friends/sports/clubs/etc!" Fill in what it is you're TOO BUSY to learn right now that you wish to learn or know you need to learn someday. Here are some ideas: computer programming, building a Web site, algebra, foreign language, music . . .

Now turn to a friend. Ask your friend to fill in what HE or SHE is too busy to learn right now.

"I don't have time to learn _____."

Now decide together when you're going to find time to fit learning that into your schedule. Maybe sooner would be better than later. You think?

Make a date with your future right here:
_____ (mm/dd/yr)

Commuting to My New School Is Killing Me!

The Problem I am in grade 6, and I go to an Arts Elementary for dance, drama, music, and art. The school is okay, but I live one and a half hours away. Every morning, I wake up at 6 A.M., drive half an hour, take City transit for an hour, and walk to my school. The same on the way home. I'm really tired when I get there, and I feel so far from home. I have a couple of friends, but I miss my best friend. I get home at 5 P.M., and I'm totally stressed. I'd go back to my old school, but everyone would think I'm a loser or a chicken, Any good suggestions?

—"E," 11

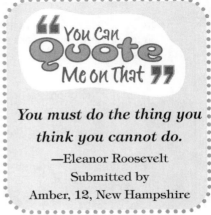

You Can Quote Me on That

You must do the thing you think you cannot do.

—Eleanor Roosevelt
Submitted by
Amber, 12, New Hampshire

A Solution Hey "E"! Ask yourself if you truly enjoy the school and the people there. If you do, I would keep on going to it! As time goes on, it will seem more and more like home! There are many other ways to keep in touch with your old friends. Go to their houses, call them when you get home, send them an e-mail, or talk to them with a computer messaging program.

As for the drive, I can only suggest taking along a good book or magazine to make the drive more interesting. If the long hours are making you tired, try to get to bed earlier so that 6 A.M. won't seem so early. You can sleep later on weekends. This "arts" school sounds cool, and I am sure that in time you will learn to love your new school and make many new friends!

—Nicole, 14, Ohio

Q. Imagine that you are in chorus at school and the girl next to you is always (and I do mean always) off key. Imagine it is driving you nutz! You can't move away from her because you both have assigned spaces. What would you do?

—Carol, 13, Rhode Island

There's no right or wrong answer. Just circle what you think. Then look over your answers and talk about them with your friends.

1 I'd tell the chorus teacher. She or he might move me or the off-key girl.

Mostly disagree   Somewhat disagree   Somewhat agree   Mostly agree

2 I'd drop out of chorus. It is not worth an annoying, off-key person.

Mostly disagree   Somewhat disagree   Somewhat agree   Mostly agree

3 I'd tell "off-key" myself. She might be mad, but at least I'd get my point across.

Mostly disagree   Somewhat disagree   Somewhat agree   Mostly agree

4 I'd ignore it. It may be annoying, but I don't want to hurt her feelings.

Mostly disagree   Somewhat disagree   Somewhat agree   Mostly agree

5 I'd suggest voice lessons. Maybe she will get the point that I am trying to make. She needs help!

Mostly disagree   Somewhat disagree   Somewhat agree   Mostly agree

I Moved into a Nest of Vipers

The Problem I just moved to a new town and it's been really hard. I mean sure, I've got some friends, but most of the kids don't like me. I don't know why because I don't even know them. People say that you shouldn't let the little things bother you, but it's hard not to. HELP!

—Jessi, 13

A Solution Dear Jessi: It's tough moving, and I know because not too long ago I did the same thing. You feel like you don't quite fit in anywhere and nothing is the same. It's a whole new world, minus your friends, and, yes, the little things bother you.

I found that often YOU have to make the first step to making new friends. The girls who don't like you don't know you. Try to make small talk with them, and let them get to know the real you. Join in on group activities, and if you're having a really hard time, talk to a teacher you like and trust. Things will work out; it just takes time.

Try to keep a journal of your experience. For example, Today so-and-so smiled at me and we talked a little bit. Little things like that are a big step ahead. Looking back in your journal will show you how far you've come and give you the confidence to move on.

Always keep contact with your old friends. They are probably just as upset by your moving. Often they can be a great support! Remember that situations like these make you stronger and prepare you for the future.

—Leshell, 13, Canada

Unpopular Kids Ignored by Teacher

The Problem Why is it that teachers don't pay attention to the nonpopular kids? I'm pretty popular, but I feel bad for those who are ignored. How can I "suggest" to our teacher that she call on some of the kids she usually ignores?

—Etoshia, 14

A Solution Hey Etoshia! That's a tricky one. How does your teacher ignore some of the kids? Not ask them when they put their hand up? Ignore them totally? Sometimes, teachers may favor pupils who they think are bright. Try and go to some of your popular friends who your teacher doesn't ignore, talk to them, and tell them about how you feel. You can't really tell your teacher that she is ignoring some unpopular pupils, but you can try and do things to make her attention go to the less popular ones.

Get some of the popular kids in class to help you. Don't actually ignore your teacher, but you could not speak to her directly unless she asks you something. This will probably give the unpopular kids a bigger chance. In class, if the teacher asks a question, you could act as if you are unsure, so don't put your hand up. She will probably ask someone else.

After a bit, she'll probably realize that not every-

"You Can Quote Me on That"

When you get into a tight place and everything goes against you . . . never give up. For that is the time and place the tide will turn.

—Harriet Beecher Stowe
Submitted by
Hilda, 17, Indiana

one is perfect, and she may start giving others a chance. Or if an unpopular kid sticks his or her hand up to answer the question, you could say "Sue (or Bill) knows," to get the teacher to call on the unpopular girl or boy. Well, hope it works.

—So Yi, 11, England

Someone I Look Up To

Kindness is not a quality you're born with but is a quality you learn to have. It doesn't come in a package, but it comes from the heart. I learned to become more generous, and thoughtful from a good friend named Tania. She showed me the true meaning of "kindness." Whenever someone needed help, she would be there. You could always depend on her when something went wrong in your life.

Tania plays an important part in my life. She showed how good it feels to change the life of another person. She showed me how it's good to help other people because one day if I need help, I'll also have someone to help me. She believes that there is an angel watching over everyone, and that sometimes the angel is someone you know. I think that Tania, with her good-hearted soul, is the angel watching over me, and many other people.

—Michelle, 13, Massachusetts

Lonely in Foster Care. Help!

The Problem I'm in foster care. I was recently moved to a new family and don't know how to fit in. What can I do?

—Perla, 14, Montana

Journalize It!

It's Your Lucky Day!

Imagine it's your lucky day! You've just won a two-hour visit with any person in the whole world. You and _____ (fill in the blank with the name of that lucky person) get to be all alone, to talk about anything.

What would you like to say to that special person?

What would you like to hear this person say back to you?

Because of that meeting, what happens next in your life? Anything special?

Now have some fun. Ask a friend to imagine their dream meeting and answer the same questions.

What would your friend like to say to her (or his) special person?

What would your friend like to hear this person say back?

Because of their meeting, what happens next in your friend's life? Anything special?

A Solution

Hey Perla! It can be so difficult to move in with a new family you barely know. But at the end of the day this family has agreed to take care of you, so you should try and appreciate what they have done for you. Maybe you could try and talk to them and tell them how you feel. Maybe they have no idea how you feel. They might make an effort to make you feel more at home. My best friend is also in foster care, but she makes an effort to try and get to know her new family. It can be hard, but try and make an effort. Maybe you could do some activities your new family does just to get to know them. This will give them a chance to get to know the real you.

Why don't you try and make some friends so you have somebody to talk to. I just moved and felt so lonely leaving behind my closest friends. But then, just to meet new people, I took up kick boxing, and that's where I met my best friend. You could join youth clubs or take up a sport you enjoy. Either way you'll definitely make new friends; I'm sure soon enough you'll fit right in.

—Angelina, 14, United Kingdom

I Can See the Horizon

I can see the warm light,
Beckoning me forward,
Calling me.

I try to run closer,
But the faster I run,
The farther away the light gets.

Finally, darkness shows its ugly face.
It snickers and snarls at me.
I collapse, and start to hope against all hope.

I wish for the darkness
To hurt me no more,
And I can see the horizon.

—Written by Nina, 15, Australia
Edited by Laura, 17, California

Someone I Look Up To

Before I got to high school, I was the best. I was the one looked up to in the saxophone group in my grade, and I enjoyed every moment of it! Once I started high school, however, I was combined with not only 10th grade but 11th and 12th graders also. I was no longer the best and no longer looked up to. The first-chair saxophone player and I didn't get along at all during the marching band season. We argued a lot! Finally, I gave up and decided not to say anything to him at all. I thought, "Hey, he's a senior and will graduate this year, so I won't have to put up with him after that!" I had struggled with my playing ability through the months following and seriously needed help! The music was getting harder, and I couldn't play it.

Let there be kindness in your face, in your eyes, in your smile, in the warmth of your greeting.
—Mother Teresa
Submitted by
Star, 14, USA

Later, in March, that same sax player had no music in band, and I was the only one there that day who played the same music he did. Trusting my instinct, I slid over and shared with him. We got into a nice, friendly conversation. He asked me if I needed help in my music, and I told him I could use all the help I could get. For the rest of the year, he helped me once a week after school for an hour, and we became REALLY

GOOD friends. He had taught me not only how to be a better player but also a lesson on friendship, which I know has changed me forever. He taught me to give people a chance and to not judge them by your first impression.

It was really sad to see him graduate, simply because I knew that the following year when I started school he wouldn't be there. We now are really close friends, and although miles separate us, we hold each other in our hearts.

—Celia, 16, New York

A Broken Leg Meant Attention.
Now It's Healed and I'm Ignored!

The Problem I broke my leg and had to spend most of the summer in a cast. I got so much attention that I pretended that my leg still hurt so I could keep it on longer. I know this is wrong, but the cast is now off and nobody pays any attention to me anymore. I don't want people to feel sorry for me, just to know I'm alive. What would you do?

— Donna, 15, Mexico

A Solution Hey Donna! I know how you feel, about no one knowing you are alive! I don't think you want "sympathy" attention

You Can Quote Me on That

The secret of being tiresome is to tell everything.

—Voltaire
Submitted by
Sherri, 16, Illinois

Q. Everyone at school thinks I'm snobby but I'm just shy. I want friends. If you were me, what would you do?

There's no right or wrong answer. Just circle what you think. Then look over your answers and talk about them with your friends.

1 I'd start slow. I'd make one new friend by starting up a conversation.

Mostly disagree   Somewhat disagree   Somewhat agree   Mostly agree

2 I'd have a party and invite all the kids who think I am snobby. I'd prove them all wrong.

Mostly disagree   Somewhat disagree   Somewhat agree   Mostly agree

3 I'd try hard to look at people in the halls and smile.

Mostly disagree   Somewhat disagree   Somewhat agree   Mostly agree

4 I'd find other shy kids and make friends.

Mostly disagree   Somewhat disagree   Somewhat agree   Mostly agree

all the time, though. Well, most people notice change in people, and their appearance. Maybe, to try to get attention, you could change your style or hair. Wear something that is different from what you usually wear, and everyone will ask if it is a new outfit or "look." That might start a conversation that will lead to more fun with friends!

If that doesn't work, you could try to be nice to everyone and stand up for yourself. I know that I am shy. If you are, try not to be.

Join a club at school this fall. Volunteer for various activities and be helpful to everyone. They can't help but notice if you are out there participating in lots of activities. I hope my advice was helpful.

—Suzanne, 14, Florida

Someone I Look Up To

The person who has changed my life the most is my mom, Marlies. She has been with me through many tough times, and she's like one of my best friends. I can talk to her about anything and I'm lucky because a lot of kids don't have that. Even though we don't have a lot of money, she makes me feel like the richest girl in the world. When I was two years old, I had surgery on both feet and went through a lot of pain and was in a wheelchair for a while. She was there for me every minute of every day and encouraged me to be strong through my tough times.

Now I'm 13, and she gives the best advice about everything—boys, friends, school, etc. We just moved, and I was disappointed at first, but I talked to my mom first, and she has helped to make me feel so comfortable living in our new town that I don't want to leave. She has gone through some very tough times and has managed to stay strong and encourages other people to do the same. She helps out in our church, schools, and community. She has touched so many people's lives and she doesn't even realize it. I want her to know that I love her and thank her for all that she's done. She's a great mom; everyone should be lucky enough to have a mom like her.

—Chanelle, 13, Indiana

Hope

What becomes of a flame,
When winds blow upon it?
When it is dropped into the wilderness?
When it is forgotten by mankind?
Left all alone?
Taken apart?
Not fueled?
And what becomes of a person,

Destroyed by life?
 Dropped to the knees?
 Forgotten?
 Left behind?
 Ripped up in shreds to be thrown
  away?
 And tamed in all yearnings?
 The person finds the flame,
 Heals it,
 Brings it life,
 And the flame burns brightly,
As it brings
Desire and fires up
The hope.

—Written by Anya, 14
Edited by Tiffany, 11,
Canada

(About reading) Here, no barrier of the senses shuts me out from the sweet, gracious discourse of my book friends.
—Helen Keller
Submitted by
Nora, 15, South Africa

Popular Kids Keep Picking on Me.

The Problem I get made fun of all of the time. The kids at school are so mean that they make me cry. They put gum in my hair and call me names just because I'm not popular. They won't stop, and because of them I get depressed. I told my principal, but they still haven't stopped. I don't know if I should ignore them (which is hard to do) or tell them off. What should I do?

—Kristin, 13, California

A Solution Hey Kristin! This is really hard to give advice on. Although most adults would say just ignore it, I'd rather go in a different direction ('cause I know it is impossible to ignore!). It makes me SO mad when I hear about school kids being mean to other school kids. They just don't realize how detrimental it is to someone's life! I wish that when I was younger and people made fun of me that I would have done something about it. I'm not condoning fighting, that is for sure! But if you get in trouble or kicked out of school for standing up for yourself, then the person you're fighting with probably will get kicked out too (especially if the person has been taunting you, and you can prove it since you told the principal about it before).

We are stardust, we are golden, and we've got to get ourselves back to the garden.

—Joni Mitchell
Submitted by
Caitlin, 14, Michigan

If the kids who hurt you get in trouble, then maybe their parents will finally take action and those kids might leave you alone. I'm NOT telling you to go fighting anyone. I'm just telling you not to be scared, okay? When they make fun of you or call you names, you just have to come up with something to say back that is better than what they said. When they see you get sad about it, it just makes them feel more powerful over you.

If they make fun of you, then you point out to everyone how that person must not have any life at all if they want to waste their time picking on someone defenseless like you. Tell them that just because they are spoiled brats, they don't have to take it out on you. Say that the only reason they feel the need to intimidate you is because they feel insecure, and they think if they put you down then people will think they are something great. If they were such terrific people, then they could figure out something more creative to do with their time than pick on you.

I also think that you should talk to your guidance counselor and make sure to tell him or her that this is interfering with your school work and makes you depressed. Basically, this is the advice I wish someone would've given me when I was in the same situation. Just remember, just because people make fun of you, it doesn't mean your life is ruined. Nothing lasts forever. You aren't the loser; they are. Someday you'll be way better off than they will be. Don't be intimidated by them!

—Rachael, 17, Florida

Wishing I Were Different

I Goofed Up in Public. Now My Confidence Is Shot!

The Problem Our class had a talent show. I didn't know my talent, so I asked my mom for suggestions. She told me to sing a "Spice Girls" song entitled "Who Do You Think You Are?" I practiced really hard. When I was about to perform, I decided to cancel my performance, but the teacher didn't allow me. When I sang the song, it totally made my classmates giggle. I was so EMBARRASSED!

I didn't know what to do. I just went back to my seat and pretended I didn't do anything at all. From that moment on, I decided never to sing in public again. How can I regain my courage?

— Embarrassed, 12, USA

A Solution   Hey "Embarrassed"! I understand you totally! This has or will happen to everyone! But you can't let it bring you

41

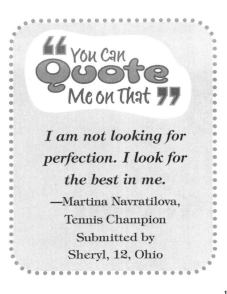

down. You can't become publicly afraid! Just tell yourself it doesn't matter and it happens to everyone. Say it over and over again! And then just sit there and think about other times someone else you know has been embarrassed so you know you aren't alone!

And don't think about it anymore. The more you think about it, the more you get hurt physically and emotionally. So it never happened! If you like to sing (in private), then you can get rid of your public fear by singing in a group (there's comfort in company), or practice by first singing for just a few good friends you know won't laugh at you.

To tell you the truth, something similar happened to me before. Five of my friends and I did "Wannabe" by the Spice Girls. I did a cartwheel and accidentally kicked my friend in the face, and my skirt went right over my face! Even worse, my BF was there! But cheer up! Goofing up a song was not as bad as me being a total spaz!

—Keely, 13, New Hampshire

The Day I Dread

Oh no! Help! The day is here!
The day of fright, the day of fear!

What is it? I'll tell you now,
It's the school concert, anyhow!
Some kids may not be scared;
It doesn't matter, it's the day I dread.
Acting as a Mom doesn't really gleam,
I had much smaller parts in my dream.
What if I giggle and wander about?
What if, accidentally, I begin to shout?

I bet that I'll have a laughing fit,
Right in the middle of the candy shop skit!
I hope I won't forget my clothes,
Or recite words which nobody knows!
I hope the stars are sick today,
So that we won't have to perform anyway!

—Written by Rachel, 11, Australia
Edited by Jessi, 11, Kentucky

Someone I Look Up To

I have a special person in my life, and her name is Cindy! She was my old dance teacher. She brought the light out in me and taught the meaning of life and why we should treat every day like it might be our last! Cindy also said that smiles make everyone feel better. So now I know that to make someone feel better, the key is laughter and smiles!

Then Cindy closed the studio! I was devastated! I really thought she was the wind beneath my wings and made me fly like a

You Can Quote Me on That

When I look into the future, it's so bright, it burns my eyes.
—Oprah Winfrey
Submitted by
Kayla, 12, USA

Q. I was on a dance team in 2nd, 3rd, and 4th grades. I am in 6th now and I want to rejoin, but I don't know if I can still do this. I don't want to mess up in front of the whole town and be embarrassed. Should I try to rejoin the group? What would you do?

— Andreanea, 12, Japan

There's no right or wrong answer. Just circle what you think. Then look over your answers and talk about them with your friends.

1 I'd just go over the old routines I remembered. I'd practice, then go for it!

Mostly disagree   Somewhat disagree   Somewhat agree   Mostly agree

2 I'd ask some of the kids in the group to practice with me before I tried to rejoin.

Mostly disagree   Somewhat disagree   Somewhat agree   Mostly agree

3 I'd ask the adult teacher or leader of the group to refresh me on the steps I'd forgotten.

Mostly disagree   Somewhat disagree   Somewhat agree   Mostly agree

4 I'd take private lessons that the group doesn't know about, then arrive a star!!

Mostly disagree   Somewhat disagree   Somewhat agree   Mostly agree

5 I wouldn't worry about "messing up." Everybody does, and I shouldn't be embarrassed if it happened to me.

Mostly disagree   Somewhat disagree   Somewhat agree   Mostly agree

butterfly! I will always love her and treat her like a sister-mom-friend! She will always have a part in my heart!

—Jenna, 11, New York

What Do All Those "Bad" Words Mean?

The Problem At my school there is a group that always uses bad language. I know I'm not supposed to say those things, but not using basic bad language leads to not knowing what other bad language means. I often get teased for not using or knowing that sort of language. What should I do?

—Laura, 12, Australia

A Solution Hey Laura! I know this may not be exactly what you want to hear, but is it really important to you to know the meanings of those kinds of words? People who use that kind of language are usually not the kinds of people you would like to be associated with. If I

BAD LANGUAGE

Why do some kids use bad language? This Web page is all about why curse words harm. They're just words, right? If you have a friend who has no idea why everyone is so upset over a few "bad words," sit down and check out this page. At least you can show your friend why everyone is so unhappy with her or his language skills.

http://preteenagerstoday.com/resources/articles/foulmouth.htm

Try Out a New Role!

Want to change parts in the play of life? Pretend you're an actor. Let's say, for example, that you've been hired to play the role of the Coaches Assistant. Think about how you'd portray your character through things like these:

> *Your clothes/accessories*: Sports uniform, athletic socks, sport shoes with cleats, stop watch, hat, sun glasses, clipboard with schedule on it.

> *Your actions:* Knowledge about the rules, warmups, how to get the best performance. You'd be organized, excited about the game.

> *What you'd do:* Support the coach and the team any way you could.

Remember that new role at school you wanted to try out? What would you need to wear/do/act like to be believed in this new role?

I'd wear this:

I'd speak like this:

I'd act like this:

were you, I would not worry about the meanings of those words, and definitely not use that kind of language yourself!

If you are really still curious about the bad words, it would be better to tell your parents or an older sister or other adult what these kids are saying and ask them what the words mean. Tell your 'rents that you don't plan on using the language, but you feel dumb when you don't even know what these kids are saying.

—Nicole, 14, Ohio

Speak up and speak out. Women are shy about speaking. My motto is to say it—say it again, only louder and with more firmness. Then say it again with a smile, but don't flinch.

—Barbara A. Mikulski, United States Senator, Maryland Submitted by L.G., 13, Maryland

Hurt Feelings Don't Stay . . . But They Don't Go

Step on a riverbed and stir up the mud.
The sand will settle as the stream trickles on.
But never again will that place be untainted.
That is me and so it be
A river flowing
On
and
On.

—Written by Tamira, 14, Belgium
Edited by Margaret, 16, Arkansas

Q. I'm 15 and flat as a board. I want to look more like a woman, and my mom said I can have implants if I want them. I don't know much about them, and I'm a little scared. What would you do in my place?

There's no right or wrong answer. Just circle what you think. Then look over your answers and talk about them with your friends.

1 I'd say that 15 is still young. I might still "develop." So I'd just wait.

Mostly disagree   Somewhat disagree   Somewhat agree   Mostly agree

2 This is a BIG decision. I'd do tons of research on the pros and cons before ever even considering it.

Mostly disagree   Somewhat disagree   Somewhat agree   Mostly agree

3 I'd think that I am great the way I am. A big "chest" doesn't make me or anyone else a "woman."

Mostly disagree   Somewhat disagree   Somewhat agree   Mostly agree

4 I'd try to find other teens who have had the surgery and ask if it made a difference. Are they happier? What was it like?

Mostly disagree   Somewhat disagree   Somewhat agree   Mostly agree

5 I'd ask my girlfriends what they all think about it. Would they do it? Then I'd decide.

Mostly disagree   Somewhat disagree   Somewhat agree   Mostly agree

Q. I have to give a speech and I'm terrified! I'm fine giving the speech to my family, but thinking about all those kids in my class listening makes me turn to Jello. If this was your problem, what would you do?

— Colleen, 11, Michigan

There's no right or wrong answer. Just circle what you think. Then look over your answers and talk about them with your friends.

1 I'd practice and give the speech to my best buds first.

Mostly disagree Somewhat disagree Somewhat agree Mostly agree

2 Before my speech, I'd ask my teacher (after class) to give me tips on how to get over speaker's fright.

Mostly disagree Somewhat disagree Somewhat agree Mostly agree

3 If there was a kid in my class who is really good at speaking, I'd ask him or her to give me some tips.

Mostly disagree Somewhat disagree Somewhat agree Mostly agree

4 I'd go ahead and give my speech. But during the speech, I'd picture my best friend or mom in the audience and just pretend I am talking to them.

Mostly disagree Somewhat disagree Somewhat agree Mostly agree

I'm Called "The Loser," and It Stinks!

The Problem This girl called me a real bad name, but I don't swear so I couldn't give a comment back. Everyone started laughing at me. Now I'm called "the loser." Man, it stinks. What can I do?

—Amy, 12, Minnesota

EATING DISORDERS

Eating disorders, like anorexia, can be very dangerous. They can hurt or kill you, or a friend, or people you love. Here's a great resource written as a part of the "ThinkQuest" project that is all about anorexia, bulimia, and binge eating. Check it out if you don't know what to say to someone who needs help.

http://library.thinkquest.org /27755/

A Solution Hey Amy! The best thing to do when anyone calls you a name or spreads rumors is just to ignore it all. Don't cry or act as if the person's comment even bothered you. I know that it might be a hard thing to do, but nonetheless it is the best thing to do. Sooner or later, hopefully sooner than later, people will realize that you just don't care anymore, and it will all pass over.

You are not a "loser" because you don't swear! I honestly don't get why so many people think it is cool to use bad language. I think that it is just a dirty habit. I know it is hard to get laughed at, but just ignore it. People probably just thought that they would look cool if they laughed at whatever she called you. When they see that you aren't affected by it or just think it's "silly," they'll have nothing to laugh at. I hope that things get much better for you.

—Jen, 14, Washington

Q. At discos, people make fun of the clothes I wear and I'm always a wallflower. Slow dances at discos have become practically a phobia for me. Please help. What would you do?

— Kathleen, 12, Malaysia

There's no right or wrong answer. Just circle what you think. Then look over your answers and talk about them with your friends.

1 I'd check out what everyone else is wearing and copy them. I'd also practice slow dancing with a relative or guy friend until I was comfortable.

Mostly disagree   Somewhat disagree   Somewhat agree   Mostly agree

2 I'd wear my own style and walk up to a guy I'd like and ask him to dance a fast dance first.

Mostly disagree   Somewhat disagree   Somewhat agree   Mostly agree

3 I'd find a friend who dances a lot and ask to borrow some of her clothes. I'd get her to teach me how to slow dance with ease.

Mostly disagree   Somewhat disagree   Somewhat agree   Mostly agree

4 I'd go to the disco with girlfriends and, together, walk up to a group of guys and ask them to slow dance.

Mostly disagree   Somewhat disagree   Somewhat agree   Mostly agree

5 I'd say forget all that slow dancing! I'd get out on the floor with a big group of kids (boys AND girls) and boogie to fast dances!

Mostly disagree   Somewhat disagree   Somewhat agree   Mostly agree

Q. All my girl pals are into the latest fashions. Whether they buy a name-brand or from a department store, it's gotta be spandex, crop top, and TIGHT. I'm not extremely large, but I have a large waist and a "belly." This stuff looks horrible on me. If it was your problem, what would you do?

— Danesha, 14, New York

There's no right or wrong answer. Just circle what you think. Then look over your answers and talk about them with your friends.

1 I'd try to find alternatives like pants that fit nicely and a looser top that doesn't show your waist and tummy.

Mostly disagree   Somewhat disagree   Somewhat agree   Mostly agree

2 I'd think that it is way harsh for your girlfriends to expect you to wear what they wear. I'd remind them that I don't like them for their clothes and they shouldn't only like me for mine.

Mostly disagree   Somewhat disagree   Somewhat agree   Mostly agree

3 I'd start my own style trend. I'd wear clothes that I feel comfortable and "pretty" in and just ignore my friends' wardrobes.

Mostly disagree   Somewhat disagree   Somewhat agree   Mostly agree

4 I'd tell them that I just can't wear those types of fashions and ask them to go with me to find a pretty alternative.

Mostly disagree   Somewhat disagree   Somewhat agree   Mostly agree

5 I'd ask my mom or another adult who is built like me to give me some fashion pointers.

Mostly disagree   Somewhat disagree   Somewhat agree   Mostly agree

They Stare and Whisper Because I'm Different.

The Problem

I get teased and stared at in school because my mother is North American so I'm only half Arabian. The Arabians (just about everyone in my school) stare and whisper and point. I think it's rude, but what can I do? Anyone got an answer?

—Susan, 13

A Solution

Hey Susan! I know exactly how you feel. Sometimes, people tease me because they say I have a weird name. They are only doing this because they think you are different. Always remember that you should be proud of whatever nationality you are, whether you are black or white. If you make them think they are getting to you, they will stare even more.

They don't know what you are like; if you get to know some of them better and become friends with them, they may realize that they shouldn't judge people by what they look like. It's what's inside that counts. People may think that because you are not fully Arabian, you are weird. Prove them wrong! Stand up for yourself! If you get along with them, they might feel bad that they were saying horrid things behind your back. Make some friends who will help you and stick up for you!

—So Yi, 11, England

HOW YOU LOOK

Feel like all people care about is how you look? A bunch of great girls over at New Moon Publishing decided to do something about that. They started the "Turn Beauty Inside Out" campaign. Their message is simple: Girls can change the way advertisers portray girls in advertising. Let advertisers know that what they say about girls and how they say it is important to you. Here's where to go to get involved.

http://www.newmoon.org/TBIOD/tbio_poster.htm

Q. I'm going into high school this year, and in the girls' bathrooms there are no doors on the individual toilet stalls. I mean, it's really gross—people can look right in and see me when I'm in there. I need privacy. What would you do if this was happening to you?

—Heather, 14, New Jersey

There's no right or wrong answer. Just circle what you think. Then look over your answers and talk about them with your friends.

1 I'd talk to my parents and get them to get other parents to go to the school board about it.

Mostly disagree   Somewhat disagree   Somewhat agree   Mostly agree

2 I'd get other girls to sign a petition about it and present it to the school board.

Mostly disagree   Somewhat disagree   Somewhat agree   Mostly agree

3 I'd get over it. We're all girls in the girls' room.

Mostly disagree   Somewhat disagree   Somewhat agree   Mostly agree

4 I'd go before school and at lunch somewhere else more private.

Mostly disagree   Somewhat disagree   Somewhat agree   Mostly agree

5 I'd talk to my favorite female teacher about it.

Mostly disagree   Somewhat disagree   Somewhat agree   Mostly agree

I Look More "Mature" Than Others in My Class.

The Problem

I am only 13, but I have the body of a young woman. I also look more mature, since I'm the only girl in class who plucks her own eyebrows, I wear more makeup, and I wear a woman's size 9. Most of the girls in my class won't hang out with me, after they see how I look. I feel all alone. I am getting more and more depressed. These girls don't understand that I'm really a shy girl. What should I do?

—Hilarie, 13, Utah

A Solution

Hey Hilarie! One thing I want to say is do you have to wear as much makeup as you do? Sometimes less is more, meaning you can just use as much as you have to so that you can cover up any acne problems or other flaws, and maybe a little eye shadow or a light-colored lipstick, and that's it. You don't have to try to

HEALTH MATTERS

Being overweight is tough. But sometimes, kids and teens think they are overweight when they are not. Do you ever wonder about your body size? Check out this Web site at Kidshealth.org for a possible answer to your question: Am I fit or not?

I cannot and will not cut my conscience to fit this year's fashions.

—Lillian Hellman, Playwright and Author of *The Children's Hour*
Submitted by
Elaine, 13, Washington

Q. I told a well-to-do friend I met last summer at camp that my family was rich and she believed me. Now she's coming to town to visit relatives and wants to come over to my house. Needless to say, we are far from rich. What would you do if this happened to you?

There's no right or wrong answer. Just circle what you think. Then look over your answers and talk about them with your friends.

1 I'd just make a date to meet her somewhere instead of having her come over to my house.

Mostly disagree   Somewhat disagree   Somewhat agree   Mostly agree

2 I'd have her over and tell her that, to me, "rich" means rich in love, and my family has plenty of that.

Mostly disagree   Somewhat disagree   Somewhat agree   Mostly agree

3 I'd just tell her I was sick and can't see her because she might catch my cold.

Mostly disagree   Somewhat disagree   Somewhat agree   Mostly agree

4 I'd tell her I was rich, but my dad lost his job.

Mostly disagree   Somewhat disagree   Somewhat agree   Mostly agree

5 I'd tell her the truth. She's welcome to come over, but since I wanted her to like me, I lied. My family and I aren't rich. If she still comes over, then she's a true friend. If she doesn't, I don't need her.

Mostly disagree   Somewhat disagree   Somewhat agree   Mostly agree

look just like other girls, but tone it down a little and it will be easier to fit in. People are afraid of people who make them feel uncomfortable. Let these girls know you are friendly. You should try and get to know these people who are judging you by your cover, so to speak.

I know it will be hard because, as you said, you are shy, but it might be a way to get over your shyness. You will hopefully have new friends, and people will know you a lot better. Don't get depressed over this, that's for sure. Try your best to get to know these kids a little bit better, so they will get to know you better, then at least you will know you

" You Can Quote Me on That "

Dreams are necessary to life.

—Anaïs Nin
Submitted by
Kathleen, 14, California

have done your best to take care of the problem. And now it is up to them to do their best to get to know the real you. Hopefully I have helped!

—Jen, 14, Washington

Older Kids Think I'm a Baby.

The Problem Even though I look my age, some older people think I am younger and treat me like I can't do anything. Have you any advice to make me look older?

—Charity, 12, California

A Solution

Hey Charity! I have always found that attitude is everything. A good one can make or break any situation, and in your case, it may help you beyond what your looks can do. By proving yourself to be mature and responsible in your actions and attitude, people are more likely to treat you as an adult.

Some suggestions on being more responsible could be helping with chores around the house or always keeping your commitments. Prove to these older "people" that you CAN do things like kids your age. So rather than attempting to just look older by wearing makeup or high heels, try to make yourself a better, more responsible person, and you will receive the respect you want.

— Karla, 17, California

You Can Quote Me on That

Give the world the best you've got and you'll be kicked in the teeth. Give the best you've got anyway.

—Mother Teresa
Submitted by
Jessica, 15, Colorado

My Classmates Laughed at Me!

The Problem

I had to say a poem in front of my class and I made a whole lot of boo-boos. Everyone was laughing and giggling at me. What do I do so I don't get laughed at? Why are kids so cruel? Will they ever forget about it?

—Heidi, 9, Maine

A Solution

Hey Heidi! Kids are sometimes cruel, but it will pass as they get older. They will forget. You just have to remember that everyone makes mistakes, and you cannot stop them because people cannot be perfect. In fact, I too have made mistakes while reading things aloud in class, but no one remembers the next day.

Sometimes kids are cruel like this because they know it could happen to them, and they want to get a chance to laugh at others to even the score. It's not right, but that's the reasoning. This will pass at school. Something else will take the kids' attention away. Just remember how you felt when you were laughed at, and try not to laugh at other people when something happens to them.

—Suzanne, 13, Florida

FACTS ABOUT BRACES

Worried about your braces? Wonder why you need to get them? Are there any famous people with braces? What if your braces hurt? This site has a lot of good facts and fun information.

http://www.bracesinfo.com/famous.html

Where I was born and where and how I have lived is unimportant. It is what I have done with where I have been that should be of interest.

—Georgia O'Keeffe
Submitted by
Kristy, 12, United Kingdom

My Mom Makes Me Dress Like a Dork!

The Problem   My parents want me to wear skirts that come to my knees and shirts that have sleeves. But I want to wear sleeveless shirts and mini-skirts. When my friend lent me a spaghetti-strapped shirt and a short skirt, my mom saw me and freaked, and I had to change clothes. What do I do?

— Michelle, 11, North Carolina

A Solution   Hey Michelle! I am 14 years old, and I am in 9th grade, which means high school. Believe me. You do not want to wear mini-skirts and spaghetti-strapped shirts. You will be known as someone you don't want to be. It might look really nice and cute when you go out somewhere and see all of these girls dressed in what you want to wear and guys hanging all over them. It is not fun. They look at those girls as being easy, if you know what I mean. You do not want to be like them.

Even though no girl wants to be like that, you should try for a compromise. Talk to your mom about maybe letting you wear skirts that come even with your fingertips when you put your hands straight down beside of you. You can also talk to her about letting you wear those cute short-sleeved dress shirts.

> **" You Can Quote Me On That "**
>
> *You will always be in fashion if you are true to yourself, and only if you are true to yourself.*
>
> —Maya Angelou, Writer
> Submitted by
> Melissa, 11, Arizona

There is one more thing. You might want to ask her politely why she wants you to wear skirts that come down to your knees and long-sleeved shirts. She might have experienced something because of wearing mini-skirts and spaghetti-strapped shirts when she was younger.

—Casey, 14, Tennessee

My Kind of Music Turns Everyone Off.

The Problem I like listening to '80s music and soft rock. The problem is when I talk about the new song from Elton John, my friends turn away and start laughing at me and say I am a dork for the kind of music I listen to. What should I do?

—Erica, 13

A Solution Hey Erica! I've got the same problem. I like the new music that only boys are supposed to like so I am punished for it. Not the way a parent punishes you, but I am always called "tomboy" and laughed at. But you know what? I don't care what

Q. My style is "big city." I moved to the country, and all the girls make fun of me! I'm just not comfortable in dirty jeans and tee-shirts every day, and I feel depressed. What would you do if it happened to you?

—Kat, 12, Texas

There's no right or wrong answer. Just circle what you think. Then look over your answers and talk about them with your friends.

1 I'd show these "girls" some fashion magazines for teens. I'd let them know where I got my style. Maybe they'd decide it's cool.

Mostly disagree   Somewhat disagree   Somewhat agree   Mostly agree

2 Part of the time I'd wear a "clean" or slightly more stylish version of what they are wearing, like flare jeans and a hip, beaded or sequined tee-shirt.

Mostly disagree   Somewhat disagree   Somewhat agree   Mostly agree

3 I'd forget it. Who cares? My style is my business. Flaunt it!

Mostly disagree   Somewhat disagree   Somewhat agree   Mostly agree

4 I'd wear what they wear to school but keep up my big city "stylin'" on weekends. Maybe they'll start asking me how I got my "look."

Mostly disagree   Somewhat disagree   Somewhat agree   Mostly agree

5 It's not worth the heartache. I'd just wear what they wear and fit in.

Mostly disagree   Somewhat disagree   Somewhat agree   Mostly agree

Q. I'm not good at anything—sports, studies, singing, dancing, you name it. How do I stop feeling that everybody at school is good at something except me? What would you do if this happened to you?

—Nancy, 14

There's no right or wrong answer. Just circle what you think. Then look over your answers and talk about them with your friends.

1 I'd take one of those simple, fun tests you can take to see what I would be good at. I'd ask a teacher or counselor if I could take one (secretly).

Mostly disagree   Somewhat disagree   Somewhat agree   Mostly agree

2 I'd think maybe I am better at quiet things like sewing, pet care, etc. I wouldn't be afraid to try all kinds of things till I found one I liked.

Mostly disagree   Somewhat disagree   Somewhat agree   Mostly agree

3 I'd say who cares if I am the best at anything or not? Then I'd just join in, do it, and have fun!!!

Mostly disagree   Somewhat disagree   Somewhat agree   Mostly agree

4 I'd ask my mom or friends who are good at what I liked to do. I'd ask their help to get better at it.

Mostly disagree   Somewhat disagree   Somewhat agree   Mostly agree

5 I'd look around at school for kids who feel like I do. Believe me, there are plenty of them.

Mostly disagree   Somewhat disagree   Somewhat agree   Mostly agree

they think. Music is something you can relate to because it makes you feel good. And if you can really get into '80s music, then let the power be with you!

Don't listen to your friends. They don't see (or hear) the music the way you do! There are all kinds of music from Classical to Hip Hop, and there is no way all kids will like the same sounds. So you do what you are doing and keep listening to your '80s tunes because you are cool the way you are, and music doesn't take that away!

—Tamra, 13, New Hampshire

I Love Softball ... but I'm Lame at It. They Laugh.

The Problem I've got a prob. I really like playing softball, but I'm not that good at it. Actually, I've only played on a team once, like in 1st grade. I got hit in the face and quit. After that, every time I play softball I get hit—on the head, the face, and the knee. I really want to play softball at school next year, but I'm afraid that everyone else will be so much better than I am and laugh at me, or tell me to go join the 7th grade team. Help!

—Becky, 13

A Solution Hey Becky! Hi. I read your letter, and you know what? . . . I was hit in the face with a softball too! It really hurts, huh! Well, my advice is try again! Don't stop something you love because of one bad thing! If you aren't very good, then practice with some friends who will be more "gentle" with the ball until you can work up to handling those fast balls! You won't get better at the game by giving up. Learn how to use a glove and protect yourself. Practice getting the glove on the ball first before you get hit. You'll get better!

—Tamra, 13, New Hampshire

IMPROVE YOUR SOFTBALL GAME!

Here's a place online where you can get skills to improve your game! There's a special "Ask the Coach" section that will answer all your baseball/softball problems!

http://www.webball.com

Things I Can't Talk About with My Parents

I'm a Total Slave Around the House Since Mom Left!

The Problem My dad treats my 12-year-old brother better than me. My mom moved out and now I have to do everything. My brother doesn't have to do anything. What can I do to make my dad understand that I can't handle all of this?

—April, 14, USA

A Solution Hey April! Why don't you try setting up a time when you and your dad can talk about the situation and how you feel? Your dad may not realize just how hard things are for you. You are all used to your mother taking care of things, and now that she is not there to do it, your dad and brother probably assume that you, being a girl, can take over her responsibilities.

We know that this isn't fair and that both your brother and your dad need to share some of the chores. No chore should be considered a "girl" chore only. However, if they are "uncomfortable" with doing what they consider to be a woman's job, ask them to do stuff like take out the trash and ask them to at least help you keep the house neat by picking up after themselves, doing their own laundry, etc.

You should talk calmly about these problems. Your dad and bro are probably just as upset about your mom leaving as you are. You need to talk to your dad without complaining or fussing or crying. Just tell him you need help.

I'm sure he just does not realize that he's left so much for you to do alone.

—Casey, 14, Tennessee

WEB watch

CHORES AND REWARDS

Feel like no one appreciates what you do? Here's one Web site that promotes giving and getting respect for chores done. Sure, it's aimed at parents. But the idea is to bring peace to the house by creating a system where everyone helps out. Check it out and show your 'rents.

http://www.choresandrewards.com/

Just a Kid

No one ever listens to me,
but I have so much to say.
Most of it is worth your while,
the rest just takes up space.
No one really knows me,
The thoughts and theories
that crowd up my head.

But it's those thoughts and theories
that make me whole.
Without them I would be alone,
drifting in the ocean of commonplace.
No one knows my future,
not even me;
but I'll assure you one thing:
I will be heard from again.
It does not matter how
or even when.
Those thoughts will make their way out.
Someone will listen.
Everyone will know
what I have to say.

—Written by Ashley, 13, Maryland

I Can Handle TV Violence.
My Parents Think I Can't!

The Problem My family thinks TV violence affects the attitudes and actions of young kids and teens. Do you think this is always true? I can't watch anything. What do I do?

—Stephanie, 12, USA

A Solution Hey Stephanie! I do think that some television violence does affect the young mind, but that's only a few, and I think you should be able to watch these movies/ shows (except for the really bad ones). Do try and tell your folks this and explain to them that you are old enough to

What Were You Thinking?

Ever hear your parents say, "What were you thinking when you did that?" Then in your heart you heard yourself say, "Why do I keep _____? All it does is get me in trouble. I hate that."

Write down what it is you keep doing that you WANT to stop doing. What messes you up? What are your friends, parents, teachers always harping about? Here are some ideas: Talking back. Making excuses. Forgetting homework, or chores, or study time. Coming home late. Spending hours on the phone.

_____ gets me in trouble because:

Now turn to a really close friend. Ask your friend to fill in what he or she keeps doing that messes your friend up. "Why do I keep _____? All it does is get me in trouble. I hate that."

This gets (my friend) in trouble because:

Decide together if what you're doing is worth the price you're paying. Parents screaming. Your future lost. Want to make a change? Vow to help each other be your best selves. You go, girl! Get busy!

understand what you should do and should not do; what is right and wrong. Show them that you are responsible enough to watch these shows. Try to convince them that they are not all bad and many deal with real life issues and teach lessons that could even help you in a time of crisis.

When approaching your parents or family, make sure they (and you) are in a calm mood to have a discussion (maybe make them a nice cup of tea!). Make sure they have the time so that you can fully explain the whole situation without leaving the tiniest detail out so they realize what an effort you have put into this and how much it really affects you. They ought to soften up under these conditions, but you must understand they are trying to protect you because they love you!

—Callan, 12, England

WEBwatch

ALL ABOUT TV VIOLENCE

Ever wonder if watching a TV show has an effect on you and your friends? "What Does the Research Show?" Check out this easy-to-read article by the American Psychological Association. Then make up your own mind. You go, girl!

http://www.apa.org/pubinfo /violence.html

I Got an "F." I'm Afraid to Tell My Parents!

The Problem I got an "F" on my social studies test. My mom said that if I get bad grades then I can't watch TV or even

You grow up the day you have your first real laugh—at yourself.

—Ethel Barrymore
Submitted by
Christina, 11 Florida

go on the Internet for two whole months! I'm afraid to let her know. What should I do?

—Lisa, 11, USA

A Solution

Hey Lisa! I know that two months seems like forever without any TV or Internet privileges. I think two months is also a little drastic. But an "F" is a really bad grade! Of course, it was only one test. It's not like you got an "F" for a final grade. I don't think you should hide it from your mom, though, because she will find out anywa. And when that happens you won't only be in trouble for the "F," but also for not telling about it.

WANT TO IMPROVE YOUR GRADES?

Everyone gets a bad grade now and again. Here's a Web page with ideas about how to improve your grades.

http://kalama.doe.hawaii.edu
/~webzine/Higdon.HTM

I'd also like to add that maybe if you didn't have any TV or Internet privileges for two months, then maybe you would have nothing to do except study. I'm sure that is the reason your mom picked that punishment and that it's for your own good.

My advice is to tell your mom about it and tell her that you plan on studying really hard for the next tests and that you understand that you'll be punished. But also add that you hope she appreciates your honesty because any other kid would lie about it, and maybe she will be more lenient with the punishment. Even if she ISN'T less severe with your punishment, at least she will trust you. Trust is something that can only be earned, so take every chance you get to gain some with your mom.

I really hope I've helped you in some way, or any other girl with the same problem.

—Rachael, 17, Florida

Not Enough Money in Our Family

The Problem   I have two brothers, and my family has no money. If my brothers get something, there's no money for me. If I get something, they have nothing. It's tearing us apart. How can we survive the "tuff" times?

—Kate, 11

A Solution   Hey Kate! I know this is hard for you; however, because you are the girl, your brothers probably feel that you get more new things than they do and that they always have to share. Have a meeting with your parents and get all the feelings out on the table.

MAKING AND SAVING MONEY

Want to know more about making money? Saving money? Setting up your own business? Check out this fun Web site.

http://www.kidsmoneycents.com/

Maybe you could work out a schedule. Decide what events or needs are coming up for you and your brothers and then work it out in advance so that if you get something this week, then one of your brothers can get something next week, and the other brother the week after that. You have to take turns, but this way everybody will get something they need eventually!

—Shatara, 16, Florida

Someone I Look Up To

The brightest star in my life is my mother. She's the one who's brought me everywhere in life. Whenever I'm feeling low, she's always there, her eyes shining with love. She's the best thing that ever happened to me. I can tell her anything, she'll just listen. She's the most beautiful woman on earth. Whenever something's wrong, she'll always find a solution to it. I can always rely on her. She is definitely my role model. She has made me the luckiest girl in the world. If it wasn't for her, I wouldn't be here today. I can't believe she's my mother. I get A's and B's for exams because of my mother.

I'm also very glad she married my father, for he is what makes me Moroccan/American. She gave me everything I need, a roof over my head and clothes on my body. And that is what makes her my brightest star.

—Jordan, 9, Massachusetts

You Can Quote Me on That

Never mistake knowledge for wisdom. One helps you make a living; the other helps you make a life.

—Unknown
Submitted by
Krissie, 10, Canada

Sometimes My Dad Gets Drunk and Drives.

The Problem Sometimes my dad gets drunk . . . and since we have such a busy schedule, he's always gotta drive us some place. I'm really shy and not the type to call some hotline. What should I do?

—Scared, 13

A Solution Dear Scared: Although it is not too uncommon, that doesn't make it any less awful for a teen who has one or more parents with substance abuse problems. Although many of us are blessed with fully functional families, there are also many whose families have problems. Before I say anything else, I just want to say that you are not alone. Many girls have the same problems, and they all feel for you.

I assume that you are not living with your mother, or that she is somehow incapable of driving you to the places you need to go. If you have older siblings, friends, or relatives who can drive, I suggest you talk to them about your problems. If they can, I'm sure they would be more than willing to help you out with a ride.

ACADEMIC RENEWAL

Many kids flunk out. It even happens to college students. There are ways to repair your academic career. It's called "Academic Renewal." Here's an article about one program. Read it. Then go to your guidance counselor and see what your school can do for you.

http://usfweb.usf.edu/ugrads /academic_renewal.htm

At this point, calling a hotline would be ideal. But if no friends and relatives can help your father with his alcohol problem, and

AFFECTED BY SOMEONE'S DRINKING?

Ever wonder what makes people drink? Wonder what to do when people are drinking and you don't want to? Ever wonder who to talk to? Alateen is an organization of teenagers whose lives have been affected by someone else's drinking. Find someone who's been there to talk to.

http://www.al-anon.alateen.org/

ESPECIALLY if he is driving under the influence or becoming abusive to you and/or your siblings when he is drunk, I understand COMPLETELY if you are shy or just too plain embarrassed to talk about your father's problem over the phone to a complete stranger.

If you have friends and relatives you can talk to about it, GREAT! Here are two excellent books written for and about teens that I would TOTALLY recommend: *Reviving Ophelia* is an excellent book written by Mary Pipher, a parent/child psychologist. It has sections about teens with problems who have visited her, and areas just to help out the reader. Another is *Girltalk* by Carol Weston, with her teenage niece to help her. It has sections on everything from your body to education, including sections on smoking, drinking, and drugs, and family.

I hope this has helped you to cope, and I hope everything turns out OK for you and your dad.

— Katherine, USA

Life

Smokin' and drinkin' you think it's a game,
It's a serious thing and it won't bring you fame.
You think you're so cool and that you know it all,

Just remember, you'll hit hard when you fall.
You're only messin' up your brain,
And bringing your family sorrow and pain.

You still don't know what you're trying to find,
The body cannot live without the mind.
You think life's a game and you can Play! Play! Play!
But you're wasting your time
    on a life that won't pay.

You think you've got every-
    thing you need right now,
Where did you get it? Why
    did you do it?
Can you tell me how?

I'm tired of the lies that I hear
    every day,
Drugs are just B.S. and crime
    doesn't pay.
Whatever you've done, it's too
    late to rewind;
The body cannot live without
    the mind!

SECONDHAND SMOKE

Secondhand smoke can kill you. Secondhand smoke is a serious health risk to kids and nonsmokers. Need information on secondhand smoke to prove that it's bad to someone who smokes?

http://www.epa.gov/iaq/pubs /etsbro.html

—Written by Jaimie, 15, Minnesota
Edited by Mei, 14, Malaysia

My Parents Want Me to Be an Exchange Student. I Don't Want To.

The Problem My parents want me to go on an exchange. But I don't want to go! Please help, and quickly before they send back the form.

—Alicia, 13

Q. My dad drinks too much and embarrasses me in front of my friends. What would you do if it were your dad?

There's no right or wrong answer. Just circle what you think. Then look over your answers and talk about them with your friends.

1 I'd never have friends over or only have them over when Dad is out.

Mostly disagree   Somewhat disagree   Somewhat agree   Mostly agree

2 I'd have a family meeting and let my dad know how I felt about his drinking.

Mostly disagree   Somewhat disagree   Somewhat agree   Mostly agree

3 I'd ask my mom to get Dad some professional help.

Mostly disagree   Somewhat disagree   Somewhat agree   Mostly agree

4 I'd confront him alone and tell him how I felt about his drinking.

Mostly disagree   Somewhat disagree   Somewhat agree   Mostly agree

5 I'd ask a minister or other adult to help him.

Mostly disagree   Somewhat disagree   Somewhat agree   Mostly agree

A Solution

Dear Alicia: Have you tried talking to your parents? Have you just had temper tantrums, or have you actually sat down and had a heart-to-heart talk?

If you sit down and discuss things rationally, then your parents are more likely to listen to you. Ask them exactly why they feel so strongly about sending you on the exchange program. When they are done talking (throughout this you sit quietly and listen), you explain why you don't want to do it.

Be sure you have some good reasons thought out already so you can "state your case" well. If your parents still insist on sending you, they have got to have a good reason. Even if you are disappointed, though, be calm. That way, next time they will value your opinion more. Good luck!

— Mariel, 12, New York

Someone I Look Up To

Whenever I needed someone to hold me and tell me it's okay, she held me and spoke softly into my ear. When all of life's little problems seemed to come all at once and I wanted to hide forever, she spoke of the future and the good tomorrow would bring. She held my hand and guided me through life and swears she will until the end. I hope she never leaves me because I love her more than words will ever express.

I'm sure she thinks, and others may too, that she is just doing her job, but it's more. It is something she does that makes it more than that. It's her—the glittery twinkle of her loving eyes, the safe security in her embrace, and the soft gentle way she whispers to me as she holds me tight. She is my mother and my bright light.

— Jodie, 12, Oregon

Q. My mom won't let me shave my legs. How do I confront her? All my friends ask me about it! What would you do if it was you?

—Helpless and Hairy, 13, Georgia

There's no right or wrong answer. Just circle what you think. Then look over your answers and talk about them with your friends.

1 I'd ask if I could get my legs waxed instead. Maybe your mom just doesn't want you to "play" with a razor.

Mostly disagree   Somewhat disagree   Somewhat agree   Mostly agree

2 I'd get a bunch of "hairless" girlfriends together and let them help me convince my mom.

Mostly disagree   Somewhat disagree   Somewhat agree   Mostly agree

3 I'd do it anyway. Once it's done, maybe my mom would like it.

Mostly disagree   Somewhat disagree   Somewhat agree   Mostly agree

4 I'd get a friend's mom who does let her daughter shave her legs to talk to my mom about it.

Mostly disagree   Somewhat disagree   Somewhat agree   Mostly agree

5 I'd just wait until my mom changed her mind. Until then, I'd wear tights that cover my legs.

Mostly disagree   Somewhat disagree   Somewhat agree   Mostly agree

I'm Black. My Foster Family Is White.

The Problem I'm Black. My foster family is White. They're really nice to me, and they let me see my real mother all the time. But there are these kids at school who make fun of me. One of them followed me home, and now I'm scared something bad will happen to my foster family. What do I do?

—Terrified and 12

A Solution Dear Terrified: Trust your instincts. If you feel something bad will happen, don't wait! Tell your parents. Tell the teachers at your school. Don't let anybody turn you into a victim!

Sometimes kids tease because they don't know what's up with you, so they make things up. Don't let them spread rumors. I have a friend who is with a foster family. It's a good thing, not a bad thing. Sometimes families need help and a break to survive. Don't hide the fact that you're with a foster family. If they think you're ashamed, they'll lay on you hard. Tell them you still see your mom and you love her. Try to pick apart the group that's making fun of you. See them one on one and talk. Be strong! Stand up to

MOVING!

It's stressful for kids and adults. This Web page is all about dealing with a move and how to adjust to a new place. The advice is aimed at parents. You can show them this page and get some ideas about how to take control of your own move.

http://www.usps.gov /moversnet/kids2.html

Q. There's a great concert coming up. I can't drive yet, and my mom won't let me go with older kids who can. What would you do if this happened to you?

—Anonymous, USA

There's no right or wrong answer. Just circle what you think. Then look over your answers and talk about them with your friends.

1 I'd ask my mom or dad to drop me off and then pick me up later.

Mostly disagree   Somewhat disagree   Somewhat agree   Mostly agree

2 My mom is cool. I'd just ask her to go and take me and my friends.

Mostly disagree   Somewhat disagree   Somewhat agree   Mostly agree

3 I'd take some kind of public transportation (bus, shuttle, subway, etc.).

Mostly disagree   Somewhat disagree   Somewhat agree   Mostly agree

4 I'd tell my mom I was spending the night with a friend, then go with the older kids who can drive.

Mostly disagree   Somewhat disagree   Somewhat agree   Mostly agree

them! When they get alone with you and see they are hurting you, maybe they will feel bad and stop.

Hang in there! Find friends who will be there for you!

—Natassia, 14, Nebraska

Divorced Mom Is Getting Married and Dad Hates It!

The Problem I have it the worst! My parents are divorced. My dad is mad because my mom is getting married again. What should I do?

—Angel, 14

A Solution Hey Angel! I think you should talk to your dad and tell him what you think. Tell him that when he and your mom got divorced, that meant that both of them decided

DIVORCE IN YOUR FAMILY?

Dealing with divorce in your family? Feel like no one understands you? Check out this Web site with your mom or dad. Talk about any issues in the article that may reflect what you're thinking and feeling.

http://www.parentingnm.com/0003dvrc.htm

to be on their own. So now your mom is free to marry again. Your dad is also free to marry (I'm just guessing), but maybe your dad is jealous because he hasn't found someone new or gotten married yet and your mom has. That's something to keep in mind when you talk to him. Good luck.

—Amanda, 14, USA

Scared to
Tell Anyone

An Older Boy Got Way
Too Fresh. I'm Scared!

The Problem This 16-year-old boy who lives down the road used to come over every day last summer. He helped me build a Web page so I kind of trusted him for a while. One day I went to his house with my brothers. I got bored and said "XXXXX, can I see your room? PLEASE?" So he led me up into this room. When we got in there, suddenly he tried to pull down my pants. I held onto them in fear as I raced out. He yelled to me as I ran down the stairs, "Hey, we still have a lot of time because they're still playing games!" Scared, I replied, "I want to watch them play!"

So I ran into the game room and sat on the other end of the room with my big brother. I don't know if I should tell my mother or what? I don't want to have her call him and then have the rest of the neighborhood boys come and rob us in revenge. I'm really scared, and sometimes I cry because I really don't know what to do! HELP ME!

— Devon, 12, Canada

A Solution   Hey Devon! You should tell your mom about the incident. Anything that happens to you that is not appropriate, you should tell your mom. She can help you and she will be a great asset to your emotional feelings. She will listen and give you advice on what to do. Your mother can talk to the boy and his parents and try to tell them what happened to you. Together maybe they can get this boy counseling help because he is taking advantage of girls and he needs to talk to someone as soon as possible!

The fact that the boys on your street would try to harm or steal from you for revenge is awful. But there's a good chance he would be embarrassed and not tell his friends about the incident at all. Even if he does tell them and they try something, it's worth the risk because this guy has to learn that he can't take advantage of girls like that. It's up to you and your parents to stop him from doing this because you may not be the last one he does it to.

— Suzanne, 13, Florida

A Stalker Is Ruining My Life!

The Problem   Someone is stalking me. He makes eerie phone calls and says for me to watch my back. One time I heard footsteps behind me in my own house. I'm very terrified. I have not slept in over a month and my grades are dropping from A's to F's. I can't tell my parents because he has threatened to kill them if I tell anyone. He says he has my house bugged. In fact, maybe he even knows I am writing this. Please help.

—Kristina, 11, South Carolina

A Solution

Hey Kristina! First of all, think really hard. When this person calls you and tells you to watch your back, does it sound like someone you know? Could it be an old boyfriend of yours who is trying to scare you because you broke up with him? The footsteps that you heard in your house were probably just your imagination. This person probably does not have your house bugged. The only way that this could happen is if you left something unlocked while you and your parents were away from your house for a long time.

You MUST tell your parents. You have to always be careful with what you do. So, just in case, to be safe, do not tell your parents about this until all of you are out of your house and somewhere else. Then they might get help from the police.

This could be a lot of things; maybe an adult is mad at your dad or mom and is being sick and taking it out on you. It could also just be a total crank phone caller who doesn't even know you but gets a sick charge out of trying to control you. Don't let him win! He's too chicken to show his face, so he isn't going to kill your parents! Together,

> **"You Can Quote Me on That"**
>
> *If I have to, I can do anything. I am strong. I am invincible. I am woman.*
>
> —Helen Reddy
> Submitted by
> Ash, 13, Canada

you and your folks can stop him. Do not worry about this so much. Go ahead and sleep. It will help you in school.

—Casey, 14, Tennessee

Our Bus Driver Winks and Gives Me Dirty Looks!

WHAT IS SEXUAL HARASSMENT?

Has any of this happened to you?

Guys staring at your body

Wolf whistles and rude comments

Someone "accidentally" brushing against you in the halls

A guy won't say no, pressuring you for a date

Sneak attacks where your body gets grabbed

What do I do if it happens to me or someone I know? This Web site has answers.

http://www.feminist.org/911 /harasswhatdo.html

The Problem I catch the bus home daily. Every day the bus driver winks at me and gives me these dirty looks. This really makes me scared. What should I do?

—Ally, 13

A Solution Hey Ally! First of all, you have to understand this is serious. The fact that somebody (a kid or an adult, a friend, a member of your family, or a stranger) makes you feel uncomfortable is not fine. You have to talk to your parents, your doctor, a teacher, or any other adult you trust. Tell this person what is going on. If the person you talk to doesn't take you seriously, talk to someone else, and do it until this stops.

It is really important to do this. If this (or any other uncomfortable situation) happens to somebody you know, tell them to talk to an adult they trust. Remember, the most important thing is your health and safety.

—Irina, 12, Argentina

My Dad Gets Threatening Phone Calls. I'm Scared.

The Problem My dad has been going to other countries a lot because of his job as a lawyer. If he says something the other side doesn't like, the next day my dad is getting angry phone calls, or even threats! It scares me. I would talk about it with my mom and dad, but I feel stupid every time I try. What should I do?

—Lexie, 10, USA

NEED SOME HELP?

Here are some guidelines that are all about how to deal with threatening, annoying, obscene, or harassing phone calls.

http://www.campuslife.toronto .edu/services/police /obscenecalls.html

A Solution Hey Lexie! Don't be scared. It is just part of your dad's job. If he says something that one side doesn't like, then of course he will get angry phone calls. Don't be scared just because of some people threatening or getting angry at him. If your dad was afraid or didn't like doing what he is doing, then he would get out of that job and do something else.

Don't be afraid or feel stupid to talk to your parents. It's certainly not weird to be upset about threatening phone calls. Go ahead and talk to them. You might be scared over nothing. Your parents will probably tell you some things that you don't realize about your dad's job. They might tell you that the reason why he gets angry phone calls or threats is because the other side is jealous of what your dad said or did. Also, most people who make threats on the phone don't have what it takes to carry them out in person!

—Casey, 14, Tennessee

Time to Go

It's time to go,
To say goodbye.
A single star
Shines in the night sky.
You give a day;
We take a night.
Down falls the star
And all its light.
The clock chimes once,
The clock chimes twice.
Magic makes it
Oh so nice.
But now it's gone
And I'm alone.
I am afraid
Right to my bone.

A single candle
Flickers in the night.
I watch with awe
At its hot yellow light.
It glows so mighty,
Yet is so weak.
The flame dies out
And burns to peak.
Time ran out,
Now it's gone.
I must go fight
The evil ones.
The darkness falls,
Shadows move.
I run away,
Afraid of the grooves
On the walls and on the floor
All around me, more and more.
They keep coming
All around.
I spy the door.
It's homeward bound.

—Written by Nikki, 12, Canada

I'm Black; He's White.
I'm Afraid to Ask Him Out.

The Problem   There's this guy in my school who is totally hot, but I'm afraid to ask him to go out with me because I'm black and he's white. What should I do?

—Nacole, 13

Q. What if no one believed you? Imagine that you've moved out into the country. It's dark and scary at night. You see someone in the backyard late one night. Your parents didn't see this person. You tell them, but they still don't believe you. You're scared. What would you do?

There's no right or wrong answer. Just circle what you think. Then look over your answers and talk about them with your friends.

1 I would ask my parents to keep watch with me one night to see if this mystery person comes back.

Mostly disagree   Somewhat disagree   Somewhat agree   Mostly agree

2 I'd go get my parents the minute I saw the person next time.

Mostly disagree   Somewhat disagree   Somewhat agree   Mostly agree

3 I'd make sure all the doors and windows are locked and just ignore it.

Mostly disagree   Somewhat disagree   Somewhat agree   Mostly agree

4 I'd ask all the neighbors if they happened to be in my backyard for any reason at all.

Mostly disagree   Somewhat disagree   Somewhat agree   Mostly agree

5 I'd keep watch. Next time the person appeared, I'd call the police.

Mostly disagree   Somewhat disagree   Somewhat agree   Mostly agree

A Solution Hey Nacole! That is a very pretty name. My advice for you is to let him know or have someone let him know you like him then wait for him to ask you out. I have a friend like you, afraid no one she likes will go out with her because she is Black. If you really feel the need to ask him out, then do. But if he does happen to say no, keep your chin held high because I know there are plenty of other guys who will think YOU are hot!

—Carri, 15, Indiana

Being Bullied!

The Problem My best friend and I are being bullied. There are these girls in our class who have been spreading this rumor about us. Last year they started to tell people that we are gay. So we went to the guidance counselor at our school. He said that they are harassing us. And he told them to stop. They did, but this year they started again. They've been saying nasty things about us. I don't know any adults that I trust to tell. And I don't talk to my parents about that kind of stuff. How do I get them to stop?

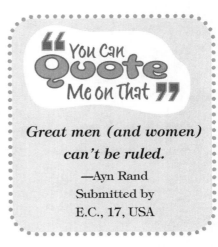

You Can Quote Me on That

Great men (and women) can't be ruled.

—Ayn Rand
Submitted by
E.C., 17, USA

—Sara-lee, 14, Canada

A Solution

Hey Sara-lee! I am really sorry to hear that you are being bullied. It is a situation nobody deserves to go through. You may have heard this before, but probably the bully feels insecure and finds bullying others a simple form of entertainment and a way of making friends, as people often try to make friends with bullies to avoid becoming the next target. I know that doesn't help, but just remember it is nothing personal. A bully's target can change from one day to the next for no particular reason. Some really nice people get bullied just because they are so nice and an easy target.

BULLIES BEWARE!

This Web site is all about stopping teasing, harassment, and threats.

http://www.bullybeware.com/

I know it is hard to stand up to a bully, but you have to tell someone. Even though telling someone last time made no difference that lasted, you have to persist. Do you have someone you trust to confide in? You say you don't know of any adults, but how about your friend, does she? Do you have an older brother or sister you could talk to or an auntie, nan, or granddad? Preferably tell your parents or another adult relative. I know you said you don't talk to your parents about stuff like this, but now is a good time to start! Your parents would probably be hurt if they knew you felt you couldn't talk to them, and they are probably eager to communicate with you but don't know where to start!

Sit them down and tell them the situation, and listen to what they have to say! If you find that they don't have time or for some other reason aren't prepared to listen, then look for another adult in your family. No relative of yours is going to stand by and let you be bullied; your problem should get sorted out in no time at all. Please speak out. It doesn't sound like it could get much worse if you are so unhappy already. I wish you lots of luck!

—Shannon, 15, England

Going to the Doctor Freaks Me Out!

The Problem How can girls face going to the doctor? With all the weird things they do, how can girls go there for physicals and such? I know it's supposed to be no big deal. People go to the doctor every day. But I'm just one who doesn't like the doctor. It's just too personal. It grosses me out. How can I get over feeling this way.

—"Anonymous," 12

You Can Quote Me on That

One of the marks of a gift is to have the courage to use it.

—Katherine Anne Porter
Submitted by
Elise, 14, United Kingdom

A Solution Hey "Anonymous"! Don't worry about it. Everyone, some time or another, gets scared of going to the doctor. Going to a woman doctor would probably help. A lot of girls prefer going to a woman doctor because they understand your body more, but it depends on the person. Some male docs are very sensitive and not "gross" at all.

When you are at your appointment, tell the doctor how you feel. Tell them that being there makes you feel uncomfortable. Ask them what is going on and what they are going to do in

Journalize It!

I Want To, But I'm Afraid . . .

Ever hear yourself say, "I really want to do
_____, but I'm afraid." Here are
some ideas for that blank: Try out for the school play,
ask that guy to the church picnic, run for class office,
write an article for the newspaper, volunteer at the animal shelter . . .

Now, turn to a really close friend. Ask your friend to fill
in what he or she is afraid to do but really wants to do
right now. "I really want to do :_____,
but I'm afraid."

Now decide together if you're willing to take the risk to
try something you really want to do. Promise to support each other if it does or doesn't work out. No, go
try it! You go, girl! Get busy!

your exam before they do it so it won't seem so weird or scary. Remember, everything you tell the doctor is confidential. Everything will be okay!

—Amie, 15, Minnesota

My Best Friend Isn't Eating!

The Problem I'm really scared for my friend. At lunch she'll never eat any of her lunch, and she'll sit there and say she's fat, but she's about 5'4" and only weighs 83 pounds! And I can't get her to eat any food because her health teacher told everyone to cut down on snacks. What should I do?! Should I tell her mom that she's on the borderline of being bulimic or anorexic?

—Ciara, 13, Ohio

FEAR OF DOCTORS

Everyone has heard of being afraid of something like dogs or spiders or flying. But many people are afraid of going to their doctor. Don't feel like you're alone. Read CBS's "Medical Minute" about "Fear of Doctors."

http://www.wbz.com/now/story /0,1597,48645-364,00.shtml

A Solution Hey Ciara! Give your friend a chance to tell her mom, but it sounds like it's already serious and you might want to take action. If she is anorexic, then her mom might have noticed it already or she might be hiding it from her. I don't know your friend, but one of my friends often does things like this and I know she's just attention-seeking.

Q. My friend has a mole on her arm that keeps getting bigger. She just ignores it, but I read that if moles change, it can be cancer. I don't want to scare her. How would you handle it?

—Chere, 16, Utah

There's no right or wrong answer. Just circle what you think. Then look over your answers and talk about them with your friends.

1 I'd tell her. I'd say whatever I had to say. Doing that might save her life.

Mostly disagree   Somewhat disagree   Somewhat agree   Mostly agree

2 I'd just ignore it. She isn't worried about it. Why should I be worried?

Mostly disagree   Somewhat disagree   Somewhat agree   Mostly agree

3 I'd ask another friend to tell her.

Mostly disagree   Somewhat disagree   Somewhat agree   Mostly agree

4 I'd talk to her mom or dad, and then let them tell her. That way she might not be as scared.

Mostly disagree   Somewhat disagree   Somewhat agree   Mostly agree

5 I'd ask my mom or dad to call her parents.

Mostly disagree   Somewhat disagree   Somewhat agree   Mostly agree

If she's that thin, however, she may not be able to stop starving herself. You might want to consider talking to your health teacher. If she's a good teacher, she'll be worried about your friend's situation too. Ask her if in one lesson she could talk about anorexia and bulimia, as they are serious health problems. If she says no, go to your principal and tell him or her what the case is and that your health teacher won't talk about it. All this talking will take a lot of courage. I don't know if I could do it, but you should try because if it gets bad enough, your friend can die!

Failure. Is it a limitation? Bad timing? It's a lot of things. But it's something you can't be afraid of. . . . the next step beyond failure could be your biggest success in life.

—Debbie Allen, Actress
and Choreographer
Submitted by
Leah, 10, USA

The Web is full of sites on anorexia and bulimia. Just go to any search engine like Ask Jeeves and type in those keywords. Hope it's helpful!

—Callan, 12, England

I'm Homeschooled. Now I'll Be in Public School in Another Country!

The Problem My family and I are moving to England, a different country. I have been homeschooled for several years. I

Q. My friend cheats all the time on homework and tests, and I can't bring myself to tell on her. Because of her cheating, she gets straight A's and gets any boy she wants. She dumped me after I bought her a $20 CD! What would you do if this was happening to you?

—Anonymous, 15, Arizona

There's no right or wrong answer. Just circle what you think. Then look over your answers and talk about them with your friends.

1 I'd write the teacher an anonymous note about my friend cheating.

Mostly disagree   Somewhat disagree   Somewhat agree   Mostly agree

2 I'd talk to the teacher after class when no one else is around.

Mostly disagree   Somewhat disagree   Somewhat agree   Mostly agree

3 I'd tell the friend's parents.

Mostly disagree   Somewhat disagree   Somewhat agree   Mostly agree

4 I'd tell my own parents and ask them to talk to her parents.

Mostly disagree   Somewhat disagree   Somewhat agree   Mostly agree

5 I'd dump her! She's just going to take me down with her.

Mostly disagree   Somewhat disagree   Somewhat agree   Mostly agree

am shy around strangers and haven't gone to public school in a long time, and now I have to go to school in a new country! I am a little scared. What do I do?

—Jennifer, 12, USA

A Solution   Hey Jennifer! So, you are moving to England? Wow, that is great! Just don't be worried about going to a public school there. You are going to make a lot of new friends, and get this: Just about everyone you will meet has never met anyone from a different country! Just this year a boy came to my high school all the way from Australia. Everyone wanted to know if he had a pet kangaroo in Australia. And everyone wanted to be his friend. So be prepared for a lot of questions.

Most of the girls you will meet will have this huge crush on the prince of England, Prince William. He is a very handsome young man in my opinion. Don't ever be scared about anything you do unless it is something that you know is wrong. Doing the things that you know are right will always lead to something great. This is a great opportunity for you to learn things that you would never learn here in the United States, and it is also a great opportunity to meet a lot of new people! Just don't be shy, and enjoy yourself there.

—Casey, 14, Tennessee

7th Grade Means More Work!

The Problem   I'm really worried about starting 7th grade because the teachers are really strict and you have tons of homework and tons of projects. My mom says I'll do fine because I made an all-A average in 6th grade, but I'm still worried! What can I do to make myself stop worrying?

—Beth, 12

A Solution

Hey Beth! Going to a different school with different people and new teachers is really scary. You don't know what it is going to be like. Seventh grade is cool and exciting, but it's going to be different. If you made A's in 6th grade, you already have good study habits. You will get through it. Usually teachers give you time in class to do some work, and you also usually have a study hall.

Here are some tips on keep your grades up:

Never fall behind because it's hard to catch up.

Do as much homework as you can in class.

Never wait till the last minute to do your homework or projects.

Don't ditch any classes.

Make a chart of your time and what needs to be done each week.

Check things off as you do them so you feel like you are making progress.

—Amie, 15, Minnesota

Out of Control

Am I Too Emotional?

The Problem I would like to know if being too sensitive is a problem in a friendship. My friends make fun of me, but jokingly. And I take it personally. It makes me mad. Could you tell me if I shouldn't be friends with them or just laugh with them?

—Rosa, 13

A Solution Dear Rosa: Being too sensitive can be a problem in a friendship. Should you dump your friends? No. Is there something wrong with you? Most likely, the answer is no.

You've probably heard it before, but when you are growing into a young woman, your shifting hormones are responsible for a huge part of how you feel. Sometimes you overreact when something bad happens. You have a lot of self-doubts. You worry about being an early bloomer or a late bloomer.

Here's a plan of action:

Don't deny that your feelings exist. There are some things you can do about getting some control over your emotions. Don't "bottle up" your disappointments. If someone has hurt you or if you've hurt them, don't pretend it's okay or didn't happen. On the other hand, if you are really hysterically happy and giggly about something great that's happened and it is annoying people, take a deep calming breath and celebrate with friends.

If you've already had your first period and you feel overly emotional, look at your calendar each month. If it's only a few days before your period, chances are hormones are greatly responsible. Keep track in a notebook of how you feel during these times each month so that you can expect and plan for these feelings.

Don't isolate yourself. If you find yourself moping around in your room, get out. Talk about your feelings with friends, your older sister, or an adult you trust. "Did you ever feel like this?" is usually answered with "Sure." Talk it out.

Join in a girl talk group with friends. Talk about problems that are making you sad, mad, or even changes that you think are cool.

My Land

Someday I'll go on a real ride;
I'll just go somewhere and hide.
It'll be an excellent place.
There won't be any dispute about race.

I'll live the life of a down-to-earth King.
I might even get a chance to sing.

I'll care about more than just some
Because no one will be acting dumb.

I'll manage a worthwhile life.
There will be no killing with a knife,
Just a little joyful play
Knowing that everything will be okay.

During this time I'll try to figure something out,
Try to find what life is all about.
But these thoughts will only last for a Moment
Because I can't wreck my enjoyment.

Maybe I'll meet a beautiful lady,
One who won't act all shady,
One who won't drive me crazy
But will keep me from being lazy.

This is all a wonderful dream
That I won't let be ripped at the seam.
But for now I'll just say a little prayer,
One for all of us to care,
For all of us to have enough
Of something to make life good even when it is rough.

—Written by Kate, 16, Illinois
Edited by Caitlin, 11, Pennsylvania

Time is the thief you cannot banish.
—Phyllis McGinley
Submitted by
Yasmin, 10, New Zealand

Sometimes it is more important to discover what one cannot do, than what one can do.
—Lin Yutang
Submitted by
Kellie, 15, New Hampshire

Journalize It!

Does Something Seem Too Hard?

Do you ever find yourself thinking or saying this? "I hate (fill in subject or activity) _____! I'm trying, but it's just too hard!"

Draw a picture in the box of one thing you could do to make that hated subject or activity easier for you.

Someone I Look Up To

My brightest star, my grandfather "Pop Pop" died a couple of weeks ago. He was my idol. I guess a lot of other people really admired and loved him, including the governor of our state and our senator. But I really loved him, and I was the only one out of all my cousins to go see his casket. My mother didn't force me either. Also, before Pop Pop, my other grandfather died, but I wasn't attached to him as much as I was to Pop Pop. I really loved him a lot.

— Teplyn, 12, Maine

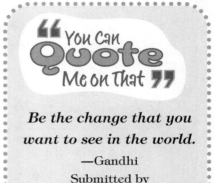

Be the change that you want to see in the world.
—Gandhi
Submitted by
Krista, 16, Georgia

I'm Plagued with Teen Acne.

The Problem I have pimples on my face. I am very scared that because of this other pupils will not make friends with me.
— Jazmine, 14, Singapore

A Solution Hey Jazmine! For most people, the decision to make friends with a person is NOT based on whether or not they have acne. However, acne can not only make you self-conscious, but it can also be painful. There are many ways to alleviate the majority of your acne or conceal it. One of the first things you may want to do is schedule an appointment with a dermatologist, or specialist skin doctor. They can give insightful

Making Changes

If you don't like something, change it.
If you can't change it, change your attitude.
Don't complain.

—Maya Angelou

Ever hear yourself saying this? "I really want to change
_____ about myself. I don't like
it. But if I change, none of my friends will like me any
more."

Fill in what it is you WANT to change about yourself
but you're afraid to change because maybe your
friends won't like you anymore. Here are some ideas:
my temper, my outlook on life, my grades, my lazy life,
my lack of confidence . . .

Now turn to a really close friend. Ask that person
to fill in what he or she is afraid to change about
themselves right now. "I really want to change
_____ about myself. I don't
like it. But if I change, none of my friends will like
me any more."

Now decide together if you'd like each other if you
made those changes. Yes? Chances are your other
friends will still like you too when you make those
changes. So you go, girl! Get busy!

tips on taking care of your face or prescribe specific medications like Retin-A crème, etc. This can be expensive, though, and there are simpler options.

Although acne can be caused by changing hormones inside young bodies, for better skin quality it is always important to wash your face. You can do this in the morning when you wake up, in the shower, and right before you go to bed. Besides washing with soap or water, there are brand name medications available in every supermarket or drugstore that you can apply on your face. A caution: Do not overuse these! Many say to use at the most once or twice a day and if used more can damage and scar your skin. Not a good idea. In any case, make it a habit to clean your face twice daily.

Another thing not to do is prod or poke at the pimples or blackheads on your face. The common belief that popping your pimples will "make them go away" is

BEDWETTING

Bedwetting is an embarrassing problem for many kids. It's usually due either to problems with bladder muscles or with difficulty in waking up. Here's a place on the Web you can go to find out more about this tough problem.

http://webmd.lycos.com /content/dmk/dmk_summary _account_1622

When anyone tells me I can't do anything, why, I'm just not listening any more.
—Florence Joyner-Kersee, Sprinter and Olympic Gold Medalist
Submitted by Tabitha, 14, California

Journalize It!

What Do You "Hate"?

Ever hear a friend say, "I hate _____
(fill in the blank with whatever—book reports, PE, Mrs.
Stilton's class, etc.). I'm trying. But it's just too
hard!." If so, fill in the blanks of the next sentence:

"Yeah, my friend _____ says that
about _____ all the time."

Now turn to a friend. Ask them to fill in what YOU say.

"Yeah, my friend (your name) _____
says that about _____ all the time."

false and can actually lead to scarring. If you've ever seen people with rather torn faces (such as Tommy Lee Jones), you'll understand what I mean. For hiding your acne, you may want to purchase a small kit of concealer makeup at your drugstore. Choose a color that matches your face and smooth small bits of it over your acne whenever you go out. Remember to wash it off when you get home. Having a concealant may give you some peace of mind. Here's a checklist to help you deal with acne.

Checklist for Dealing with Acne

❋ Scrub face twice daily.

❋ Cut down on high sugar foods.

❋ Do NOT poke acne.

❋ Rinse off your face after sports or warm periods of the day.

❋ Use a skin color concealer to hide especially prominent acne.

(Some people) deal with knots just by cutting through them. That never teaches you anything. Untying a knot teaches you because you really have to work it.

—Alice Walker
Submitted by
Melissa, 12, Arizona

Lastly, you should remember that often people with acne on their face sometimes get it on their back, shoulders, neck, and upper chest. Neutrogena and other skin care companies offer protection for these areas of your body that you can scrub with every day. You may want to look into prevention care for that sort of thing as well. Anyway, I hope your school year goes great and you make lots of friends, despite your inhibitions! True friends won't worry about a few pimples.

—Melody, 13, California

Q. Some school textbooks are so old that the "facts" no longer apply. Students are often learning outdated material. What would you do if this was happening at your school?

There's no right or wrong answer. Just circle what you think. Then look over your answers and talk about them with your friends.

1 I'd ask my teachers to update the facts before they teach each year.

Mostly disagree   Somewhat disagree   Somewhat agree   Mostly agree

2 I'd ask my parents and teachers to put pressure on the government to put aside more money for new, updated textbooks.

Mostly disagree   Somewhat disagree   Somewhat agree   Mostly agree

3 I'd start a fund-raising drive in our community to raise money for new textbooks.

Mostly disagree   Somewhat disagree   Somewhat agree   Mostly agree

4 I'd tell my teachers to dump the textbooks and learn from the Internet.

Mostly disagree   Somewhat disagree   Somewhat agree   Mostly agree

5 I'd start a student letter-writing campaign to convince local politicians to fight for more textbook funds.

Mostly disagree   Somewhat disagree   Somewhat agree   Mostly agree

Journalize It!

Ever hear yourself say, "If it's not about sports, guys don't want to talk about it." Or, "Parents just don't understand. It's just ancient history to them." We all think like that. Shortcuts. We expect groups of people to act and think a certain way. Think about guys for a second. What have you heard about "guys" as a group? Write them down here.

What have you heard about strangers? Or folks in other countries? Or old people? Pick a group. Then write down the "shared wisdom" you've heard about them.

Ready? Now ask yourself, Is this "shared wisdom" really true?

I Was Diagnosed with Cancer and I'm Scared. Help!

The Problem Please, I'm begging you, someone help me! My world is falling apart. I was diagnosed with cancer and I'm scared. I don't want to die, but I don't know what to do. Help me please!

—Kati, 12

A Solution Dear Kati: Obviously the situation you're in is not an easy one, nor will it ever lessen in intensity unless a cure is found. And right now a lot of emotions must be running through you—Am I going to die? Does this mean I'm never going to grow up to do the things other girls are going to do—like my prom or my graduation? The discovery of a serious illness often can have a devastating toll on your emotional as well as physical health. What you need to do right now is take a deep breath and ease the panic overwhelming you because, though you may feel terribly alone, the reality is—you're not. Thousands of people are diagnosed with cancer yearly, and many of them feel desperate, changed, hopeless.

Kati, the essential thing right now is that you not lose hope. Many people recover totally from bouts with cancer. Studies have

" You Can Quote Me on That "

If all the good people were clever, and all clever people were good, the world would be nicer than ever we thought that it possibly could.

—Elizabeth Wordsworth
Submitted by
April, 12, Pennsylvania

shown that people with emotional strength can often survive tremendous odds, whereas those who give up are more likely to lapse into a slow decline. Another important thing is to find information on your illness, treatment plans, and support groups in your area. The more info you know, the more ready you'll be for the battles ahead.

Below I've made a list of resources that are readily available for your use and for others diagnosed with cancer. You'll find support group listings, info on different cancers, statistics, and treatment options. Hopefully, through this network of friends, you'll begin to better understand your condition and the best way to overcome it. And another thing—don't let statistics get you down. There are little miracles all the time, and lots of kids who battle their diseases come out on top. So check out some of the Web sites and other listings below.

Cancer Help Links

Children with Cancer Resource Page
www.admins.com/~lebrun/

Why Me? Helping Children with Cancer
www.whyme.com/

Cancer Information Service
http://cis.nci.nih.gov/
or call 1-800-4-CANCER

Medicine Online
www.meds.com/

Cancer Links (Provides links to cancer sites all over the Web.)
www.cancerlinks.org/

Cancer Hope Page
http://www.shaggylamb.com/hope1.htm

Circle for Cancer Parents (Have your parents check this out!)
www.shaggylamb.com/hope1.htm

Cancer Programs for Kids
www.aspen.com/kidsstuff/dir/program.html

Childhood Cancer—A Guide for the Family
www.oreilly.com/catalog/childcancer/

Special Angels Webring—"Support for those with illnesses"
www.webring.org/cgi-bin/webring?ring=specialangels;list

Whenever you're feeling bad, try reciting this poem to yourself.

Hope is the thing with feathers
That perches in the soul.
It sings a song without a tune
and never stops at all.

—Emily Dickinson

Kati, none of us know what the future brings, but with the support of your friends, family, doctors, and online/in person support groups, hopefully you will win this fight. If there are no support groups in your state or on your Internet service provider, you might consider starting your own! If you would like to find more Web sites, go to www.netscape.com and enter in the search bar such things as "cancer," "cancer support groups," or "children with cancer." These will give you more options to choose from on the World Wide Web.

You may also be interested in talking to a counselor about the emotions that you're feeling right now. Talking to a counselor may help you better express the emotional turmoil you're going through and help you relieve yourself of the shock and pain that you feel. Another idea is to start keeping a journal and pen down those tumultuous feelings.

Whatever you do, I wish you the best of luck, love, and health in the future.

— Mel, 13, California

Dad Has Chronic Fatigue. How Can I Help?

The Problem My mother died two years ago of cancer, and our family isn't the same as it used to be. I didn't cope too well for a couple of years, but now I hardly think about it and I am coping well. But my dad has been under a lot of stress and he isn't well.

I just wish I knew what I could do so he won't be under so much stress.

—Angie, 14

A Solution Hey Angie! So sorry about your mom. That's tough. To help your dad, know that sometimes the little things can make a big difference. Chronic Fatigue can really slow a person down. Even little things around the house can really exhaust a person with the disease. Show your dad that you love him heaps, and even though your mum's gone, you're still there for him. See if he needs any little jobs done that would ease his workload and stress a bit. But the most important thing to do is for you to show him that he is loved. By you!

—Alexandra, 14, Australia

You Can Quote Me on That

We only want that which is given naturally to all peoples of the world. To be masters of our own fate. Only of our fate, not of others, and in cooperation and friendship with others.

—Golda Meir
Submitted by
Lorena, 17, Florida

Q. My best friend's mom just got cancer. My best friend is mad at me for not doing more for her. I think I've done all I can! What would you do if this were happening to you?

— Nikki, 13, USA

There's no right or wrong answer. Just circle what you think. Then look over your answers and talk about them with your friends.

1 I'd try looking up Web sites for cancer support groups, print out the information, and give it to my friend's sick mom.

Mostly disagree   Somewhat disagree   Somewhat agree   Mostly agree

2 I'd offer to help my friend with chores that will make her mom's life easier.

Mostly disagree   Somewhat disagree   Somewhat agree   Mostly agree

3 I'd help my friend find a school counselor to talk to. She's under a lot of stress.

Mostly disagree   Somewhat disagree   Somewhat agree   Mostly agree

4 I'd tell my friend that I do care and I'm very sorry about what's happened, but there's nothing more I can do.

Mostly disagree   Somewhat disagree   Somewhat agree   Mostly agree

5 I'd ask my mom what she thinks my friend's mom might like to ease her burden. Maybe there's something I missed.

Mostly disagree   Somewhat disagree   Somewhat agree   Mostly agree

I'm in a Wheelchair, and People Make Fun.

The Problem Everyone keeps on making fun of me just because I'm in a wheelchair. One time, in the cafeteria, I stopped in line to get some food and someone put my brakes on. When I tried to go, I jerked and my food fell on my new orange shoes, and people started calling me sloppy. I started to cry. What should I do?

—Klara, 12, Canada

A Solution Hey Klara! What you should do is try to get the message across that just because you are different, that is no reason for people to be mean. I know it must be hard, but people have to accept you for you. If people start to call you sloppy or other names, just ignore it. People will start to see that it doesn't matter to you what they say, and they will stop. I am sure of that.

Don't let the little things in life bother you. It is too short to get that stressed out. When people start to see that you are nice, cool, and awesome, they will start to be nicer and want to be your best friend!!! Concentrate on all the things you have in common with others, and pretty soon they'll forget any differences! They will start to see that just because you are challenged with a disability does not

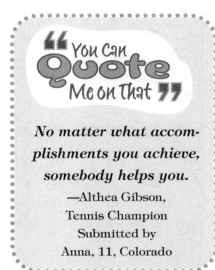

" You Can Quote Me on That "

No matter what accomplishments you achieve, somebody helps you.

—Althea Gibson,
Tennis Champion
Submitted by
Anna, 11, Colorado

Q. I have a chronic disease that makes me tired a lot, but I have good and bad days. My best friend thinks I'm sick all the time, so she doesn't ask me to go anywhere with her anymore. What would you do if this happened to you?

There's no right or wrong answer. Just circle what you think. Then look over your answers and talk about them with your friends.

1 I'd prove to my friend that, most of the time, I'm still me. I'd have an active, fun party and invite everyone who forgets to invite me.

Mostly disagree   Somewhat disagree   Somewhat agree   Mostly agree

2 The next time I heard that my friend was going somewhere, I'd just ask if I could go too.

Mostly disagree   Somewhat disagree   Somewhat agree   Mostly agree

3 I'd talk to her honestly, telling her all about my disease and the fact that I feel left out.

Mostly disagree   Somewhat disagree   Somewhat agree   Mostly agree

4 I'd give her a list of Web sites to go to that explain my disease so she could better understand it.

Mostly disagree   Somewhat disagree   Somewhat agree   Mostly agree

5 I'd find new friends locally or on the Web who have my disease and will better understand me.

Mostly disagree   Somewhat disagree   Somewhat agree   Mostly agree

mean that they should make fun of you. They will start to see that you are cool because you are who you are. Hang in there!

—Jen, 14, Washington

They Call Me "Shorty."

The Problem I'm really short. I get called names like shorty, shrimp, short-cake, etc. I've tried ignoring it, and I've tried using the saying "good things come in small packages," but none of it works to stop the teasing. What should I do?

—Tiara

A Solution Hey Tiara! Being short isn't a bad thing. A lot of famous people are barely 5 feet tall. Judge Judy, gymnast Kathy Rigby, and Elizabeth Taylor are all really short. You know all of those figure skaters? Tara Lipinski is only about 5'0". You don't need to worry about your height right now.

CLASSROOM DISCIPLINE

Have a teacher who just doesn't seem to know how to deal? Some teachers get over-whelmed by their students. Or they're new, and they don't know how to discipline. Or maybe they're just burned out. Have your parents drop the URL to this Web site off to the principal. It's got great ideas for teachers on Classroom Discipline. You can read it too for some ideas on what's expected from students like you!

http://members.tripod.com /~brimfield/index.html

There really isn't anything I can tell you that will make you feel better as long as those people are teasing you. You can't control their actions, but you can control your self-esteem. Remember that you are somebody and they can never be you. Some kids are really tall in grade school, and people call them "beanstalk" and "the jolly green giant," so it happens to both tall and short people.

In just a few years, those same boys who are teasing you will be asking you to the movies or to a dance. I promise. Always keep reminding yourself, "God made me the way I am for a reason." Like you said, good things come in small packages. The smaller the box, the more expensive the gift. Good luck and stay strong!

—Lindsay, 14, Louisiana

I Think My Friend Is Faking a "Learning Disability."

The Problem My best friend says that she has a learning disability. I don't think so, though. She has a great memory for things that she's interested in, but when it comes to school, she says that she has a disability and is excused from homework. I've tried to tell her what I think, but she always changes the subject. What do I do? At this point, she's doing so badly that she won't make it through grade 7. The teachers aren't accepting her excuse any more. They are probably thinking that if things are that bad, she should be in a special school!

—Erin, 12, Canada

A Solution Hey Erin! Maybe your friend needs to have better self-esteem. She probably has gotten herself to believe she has a learning disability. That way she knows she doesn't have to try really hard to make great or even good grades in school. Since you said she is good at remembering things she likes, you are probably right; she is just making excuses for herself not to try harder.

> **The future belongs to those who believe in the beauty of their dreams.**
> —Eleanor Roosevelt
> Submitted by
> Amanda, 12, Arkansas

When you talk to her, ask her to please listen and wait till you finish. Or you could even talk to her parents about it because you sound like a great friend to be worried about your friend. Just ask her parents if she really has a disability. If they say yes, then ask what it is. If they say something like Attention Deficit Aisorder (ADD), learn about this learning disability so you can understand how to help your friend better. You could research it on the Web and at a library. If no one is really sure she has it, there are tests for this disorder. Hope this helps.

—Suzanne, 14, Florida

My Mom Has Hepatitis C!

The Problem My mom has hepatitis C, and it scares me. What should I do?

—Ellen, 11, Canada

If I can stop one Heart from breaking, I shall not live in vain.

—Emily Dickinson
Submitted by
Nadhira, 15,
United Arab Emirates

There's two things I've got a right to . . . death or liberty.

—Harriet Tubman
Submitted by
Annie, 10, Ohio

A Solution

Hey Ellen! I know this is very scary for you, but I want you to remember that your mom is probably scared too and she is very sick. She'll feel tired and like she has the flu a lot. She needs you to be there for her. Help her any way you can because she isn't going to feel like doing everything she usually does.

Don't worry. Her doctor will take care of her and help her to get better, but it's going to take time. So the best thing you can do is help her out at home and give her all of your love. Sometimes love can be the best medicine. Take care of her like she does you when you are sick. With your help and love, she will have more time to take care of herself. My prayers are with you both.

—Casey, 14, Tennessee

Editor's Note: Hepatitis C is a liver disease caused by a virus. Hepatitis (HEP-ah-TY-tis) makes your liver swell and stops it from working right. The liver fights infections and stops bleeding. It removes drugs and other poisons from your blood. The liver also stores energy for when you need it. You get the disease from contacting an infected person's blood, like through blood transfusions (before 1992), an operation, or drug use with dirty needles. There are drugs that are effective against the disease.

Boys Think My Gal Pal and I Are TOO Close!

The Problem HELP!!! There are these boys in my class who are saying that me and my best friend are gay, and we aren't. We just can't put up with it anymore. Now, no boys like us because they think that we are. I think that they accuse us of that because I'm new at school and me and my friend do EVERYTHING together. If you did a poll, almost EVERY girl and her best friend do EVERYTHING together. Other girls in our class are that close with their best friend, but the boys don't accuse them of being more than friends. What can we do to stop the rumors?

—Mary, 12

A Solution Hey Mary! Of course best friends hang together all the time, especially if you are new at school and don't have lots of other friends yet. I think you should ask other kids if they will comment back when the boys say that. Maybe they could say something like, "That's stupid. Why would they be gay?" or "Get a life. You guys are so immature."

Sounds like these guys have just decided to pick on you. Maybe it's even because they like one or both of you and are too shy to say so, so they try to be "funny." If other kids tell them to "grow up," then the boys will feel really low. If they don't get any approval, if their friends don't think they're cool, maybe they'll stop the rumors. Good luck!

—Amanda, 14, USA

My Best Pal's Dad Is in Trouble with Police!

The Problem   My best friend's dad got in trouble with the law. I would be very uncomfortable saying what happened here, so I'm just getting right to the point. She only told a few people what happened, but still she is very out of it. She isn't as happy-go-lucky as she used to be, and I'm really surprised! What can I do to help my friend?

—Caroline, 10, Florida

A Solution   Hey Caroline! When my friends are having trouble, I try and get them to talk with me and get it out and just stand by them and see what I can do. If I can't do anything, then I just let them talk to me, and maybe in the end that is what will help them, just talking. People sometimes say that the best thing sometimes for problems is just to talk them out.

If your friend really needs help, then maybe you can talk to your parents and see what they can do. If your friend needs more help, then you might want to take her to a school counselor, trusted teacher, principal, or church group. Adults might not get some things that kids do, but I am sure that they can help you in some way with tough family problems.

Having a parent in trouble with the law is a hard thing to face. Sometimes it can be hard because you don't want people to know about it, and yet they still seem to find out. Your friend may be blaming herself for her father's actions. You want to make sure that she knows that it is not her fault that her father chose to take the actions he did. I hope that this helps your friend!

—Jen, 14, Washington

Q. Imagine this . . . what if one of your friend's parents was arrested for taking money from where they work. Now your friend is afraid to show her face at school. What would you do?

There's no right or wrong answer. Just circle what you think. Then look over your answers and talk about them with your friends.

1 Tell her that she's not her dad and she should hold her head high.

Mostly disagree　Somewhat disagree　Somewhat agree　Mostly agree

2 Tell her that you know it will be hard for her to face the kids at school, but you will be there to support her.

Mostly disagree　Somewhat disagree　Somewhat agree　Mostly agree

3 Talk to kids you know before she comes back to school and ask them to go easy on her.

Mostly disagree　Somewhat disagree　Somewhat agree　Mostly agree

4 Get your mom to talk to her mom and give the whole family support.

Mostly disagree　Somewhat disagree　Somewhat agree　Mostly agree

5 Tell her to ask her teachers if she can study at home for a while until the publicity about her dad dies down.

Mostly disagree　Somewhat disagree　Somewhat agree　Mostly agree

Worried About My World

What Can We Do About School Safety?

The Problem Do you think that there will be more violence if we got more security at school?

—Clarissa, 12

A Solution The issue of school security is a biggie, but I don't believe that one system of views can be applied to all schools; they have to be treated individually. I'm from England, and over here there is hardly any violence in schools—certainly not to the degree that there is in America.

Recently at my school we had security cameras installed on the playground, to stop people doing graffiti on the walls. Almost everyone I know, those who had and had not gotten into trouble before, felt really annoyed at this, including me. It really felt as if no one trusted us (we'd never had a graffiti problem before), and the whole building had a really bad feel about it.

BE A PEACEMAKER

We must be the change we wish to see.

—M. K. Gandhi

Check out the Gandhi Institute. This Web page is all about how to practice and promote non-violence.

http://www.gandhiinstitute.org/

People started to think: "If they think we're gonna do it anyway, we might as well do it and have some fun," and the amount of graffiti actually went up. I fear it might be the same in some American schools. However, when the problems are pupils being injured (and, in the case of Columbine, killed) rather than harmless graffiti, the people in charge of school security need to be extremely careful to make sure that the security systems are put in place for the students, and with their help, rather than to scare or intimidate them (a scared or angry student is a dangerous one, whatever country we're in). It will probably take time, but I do think that the right balance can be achieved if everyone involved really wants it.

—Janie, 15, England

More Trouble at School Means I Lose My Foster Home!

The Problem I am having problems at home with my foster parent. She says that if I get suspended from school one more time, I am out of her house. But if I leave there, I will be going to a group home. Plus I can't go back to my mother until I am 18 years old. What should do?

—Tyesha, 13, New Jersey

A Solution

Hey Tyesha! Seeing that you don't want to go to a group home and you can't go to your mother, I think you should try not to get suspended. What do you keep doing that keeps getting you into trouble? Whatever you're doing at school, just stop doing it. If you are getting pressure from your friends, find new friends. Whatever you are doing that is making the school suspend you isn't worth having to be put in a group home if you are otherwise pretty happy with your foster mother.

If it's stuff like smoking or cutting class or being late or getting involved in fights, these are things you can control. Take charge of your life! You can shape your tomorrow. It may not be as easy as I'm saying, but try. Good Luck, Tyesha! You Go, Gurl!

—Kim, 17, Canada

You Can Quote Me on That

If it wasn't hard, everyone would do it. It's the hard that makes it great.

—Tom Hanks's character in
A League of Their Own
Submitted by
Kaitlin, 15, New York

WEBwatch

VIOLENCE

Violence in teen relationships is on the rise. Here's a Web site that's all about understanding teen violence. There are links to what violence is and how to stop abuse when it happens.

http://www.maav.org/

Journalize It!

Not Old Enough to Worry?

Ever hear yourself say this? "I don't have to worry about _____ yet. I'm not old enough!"

Fill in what it is you're NOT old enough to worry about yet. Here are some ideas: boys, career, fitness, dating . . .

Now turn to a friend. Ask your friend to fill in what he or she would say.

"I don't have to worry about _____ yet. I'm not old enough!"

Now decide together when you're going to worry about it. Maybe sooner would be better than later. You think? Make a date with your future right here:

_____ (mm/dd/yr)

A Perfect World

A perfect world—
Is there a such thing?
And if there was,
What would there be?
World Peace?
Flowers Blooming?
Cures for diseases?
Will we ever know for sure?

These are questions we ask.
Right now, we have to deal
*   with what we have.*
We can't change the world by
*   ourselves.*
We'll have to work together
*   on this one.*
We can't change the future
*   either, but we can change*
*   today.*

A perfect world?
How can we make one?
Will it ever happen?
How? Why? Will? Is? If? What?
These are things we will ask. So—

Let's get ready for the future.
Let's get together,
Let's help each other,
Let's work together,
Let's come together,
Let's make this a perfect world.

PREVENTING HOME BURGLARIES

Many home burglars are kids or teens. They're not professionals. They are looking for quick money and a fast exit. This Web site tells you what kind of home is an easy target for burglars and how to make yours safe and unattractive to unwanted visitors.

http://www.sbpd.com /education/prv459.html

—Written by Brittney, 10, New Jersey
Edited by Melody, 13, California

Kids at My School Turn to Violence to Solve Problems.

The Problem Why do you think a lot of kids turn to violence as a way to solve problems, and how can we help them find peaceful ways to deal with their problems?

— Pratima, 11

A Solution Hey Pratima! There are many reasons why individual people turn to violence, but one of the main problems is a breakdown of communication between teenagers and their families—having a problem, or feeling angry, and not being able to talk about it with anyone.

WORRIED ABOUT PERSONAL SAFETY?

Here are some tips about how to protect yourself while you're walking at night.

http://www.almostheaven-lv .com/safety/assault.html

Although it's a rather sexist judgment, it is usually boys who get into fights and commit violent crimes. Boys tend to keep things bottled up so that they can look good in front of their friends. It is usually (although not always) different with girls. If we are feeling upset, then we usually feel comfortable enough to discuss the problem with our friends or close family. Most of us cry a lot more easily than boys, and we're generally not nearly as bothered about keeping up a macho image.

Another thing is that teenagers take TV and films a lot less seriously than previous generations. I have seen *The Matrix* ten times, and I think it's really cool. When my mum saw it with me, however, she was really shocked about all the guns and how much violence there was. I hadn't given it a second thought. One of the reasons so many teens in America at the moment are turning to guns and other extreme sorts of violence is that many of them don't actually realize what effect they will have in real life. In fights in films and TV, for example, and even in "Tom and Jerry" cartoons, it's not unusual for someone to get hit over the head with an iron bar, or get punched in the eye. It never looks particularly painful, and the person stands up in the next scene to throw a punch at the attacker. In a real fight, however, an iron bar over the head could very easily be fatal.

Short of banning all violence in films and TV programs, there is very little we can do to stop this kind of influence on teenagers. However, it would be a good start to begin to change the way teens look at violence—particularly the sort

WEBwatch

PREVENTING SCHOOL VIOLENCE

It's possible to prevent violence at school. There's certain signs you may see that are warnings, calls to take action. If you see a friend suddenly act like this, talk to a teacher or their parent.

- Your friend loses interest in school
- Gets angry, blows up a lot
- Hates following rules, ignores rules a lot
- Hurts pets or animals
- Talks about feeling like a victim
- Draws violent or angry pictures
- Gets totally into weapons or violent shows and games
- Gets totally depressed
- Shows up with any kind of weapon

Here's a Web site with more ideas and ways to help. It's sponsored by the National Crime Prevention Council.:

http://www.ncpc.org /2schvio.htm

Q. My friends and I disagree on how to keep schools safe. What do you think we should do to keep schools safe?

There's no right or wrong answer. Just circle what you think. Then look over your answers and talk about them with your friends.

1 We should have metal detectors at every door and make everyone pass through them every day.

    Mostly disagree   Somewhat disagree   Somewhat agree   Mostly agree

2 We should have armed guards in all the halls.

    Mostly disagree   Somewhat disagree   Somewhat agree   Mostly agree

3 We should arm the teachers.

    Mostly disagree   Somewhat disagree   Somewhat agree   Mostly agree

4 We should send troublemakers to the principal's office. Three strikes and you're out of school permanently.

    Mostly disagree   Somewhat disagree   Somewhat agree   Mostly agree

5 We should head off violence early by making all kids feel welcomed with student talks and weekends where kids from different social groups can gather and air their differences.

    Mostly disagree   Somewhat disagree   Somewhat agree   Mostly agree

of damage it causes. Here in England we have very strong weapons laws—no one is allowed to carry guns (unless the person is a farmer, etc.), laser pens, flick knives, or any kind of spray (such as CS Gas), even if it is for self-defense. In America, however, there are thousands of guns—something like one in every ten houses. It does not seem surprising, then, that there is such a huge gun problem in the States. If the weapons aren't there, then neither is the weapon problem.

—Janie, 15, England

For me it's the challenge—the challenge to try to beat myself or do better than I did in the past. I try to keep in mind not what I have accomplished but what I have to try to accomplish in the future.

—Jackie Joyner-Kersee, Sprinter and Olympic Gold Medalist
Submitted by Jessica, 15, Canada

My Best Friend Can't Give Up Drugs. Help!

The Problem I have a friend addicted to drugs. She is my best friend in the whole world. She means everything to me. I tell her she shouldn't, but she tells me its too hard to quit. What should I do to make her see my point? How can I help her?

—Kimberly, 13, USA

A Solution

Hey Kimberly! Your friend is right. It is hard to quit after you begin to take drugs, but she has to know what sort of effects drugs can have. You have to be there for her and be the best friend you can be. Sit her down and have a long talk with her, telling her how much you care, and you don't want to see her ruining her life like this. Your friend won't have the willpower to quit, but if you help her and show her you will be there for her through thick and thin, then she will know she has a friend who is there for her all the time.

You should also try and find out how and when she started drugs. Maybe she hangs out with a bad crowd. If that is the case, you should try to stop her. My brother began to take drugs three years ago, so I decided to have a talk with him. It turned out he was really unhappy. He wanted to quit, so my mother sent him to a counselor. Now he is in the best of health and very happy.

Maybe your friend feels the same but has nobody to talk to. I know you wouldn't want to betray your friend, but tell an adult. They could help you. You probably think telling an adult is wrong because your friend will get angry, but when she's finally over drugs she'll thank you for telling an adult. But do ask yourself: Would I like to help her now and see her back to normal again or see her in pain? You have to realize drugs can kill, so then you can tell her the effects they have.

" You Can Quote Me on That "

Adventure is worthwhile in itself.

—Amelia Earhart
Submitted by
Lateesha, 12, Louisiana

It's a hard fact, but if your friend carries on like this, her life could be over.

—Angelina, 14, United Kingdom

Another Voice

A Solution Hey Kimberly! Explain to your friend that her use of drugs is putting a serious strain on your friendship. Be sure that you tell her about all the health problems that come along with drug use, and let her know that no matter what she thinks, drugs are addictive and can harm her. Sure, it's hard to quit, but it's worth it to be "clean" again. If you have any friends who have gotten off drugs and now feel better, use them as examples.

When written in Chinese, the word "crisis" is composed of two characters. One represents danger, and the other represents opportunity.
—John F. Kennedy
Submitted by
Miranda, 13, Australia

Help your friend find a local drug rehab program for teens that can help her get off drugs. It may be hard to get tough with her and might cause her to stop being your friend for a while. But if she doesn't stop using these drugs, then you have got to tell a caring adult around you because your friend's health is the most important factor.

—Shatara, 16, Florida

Q. You realize that your best friend is taking drugs. You're the only person who knows. She makes you promise not to tell anyone. What do you do?

—Annette, 12, United Arab Emirates

There's no right or wrong answer. Just circle what you think. Then look over your answers and talk about them with your friends.

1 I'd say leave her alone—it's her life anyway!

Mostly disagree   Somewhat disagree   Somewhat agree   Mostly agree

2 I'd warn her that drugs are dangerous. If she doesn't listen, then forget it!

Mostly disagree   Somewhat disagree   Somewhat agree   Mostly agree

3 I'd keep quiet. I wouldn't tell anyone. I promised I wouldn't, and a promise is a promise!

Mostly disagree   Somewhat disagree   Somewhat agree   Mostly agree

4 I'd go seek advice from a school counselor, being careful not to mention my friend's name.

Mostly disagree   Somewhat disagree   Somewhat agree   Mostly agree

5 I'd say forget the promise! I can't let her ruin her life. I need to tell someone in authority (such as her parents or a teacher).

Mostly disagree   Somewhat disagree   Somewhat agree   Mostly agree

Surrounded by Druggies!

When people around you are doing drugs or getting drunk and you don't want to, what do you say to them?

—Chelsea, 11

A Solution

Hey Chelsea! If you are ever uncomfortable with anything that is going on around you, then get out of that situation. Don't let anyone ever force you into something that you don't want to do, and never let anyone believe they have control over you.

If your friends or the group that you hang out with are doing drugs and drinking and you don't want to, then don't. Remember that you are the only person who has any control over what you do. If they start to pressure you into doing things you don't want to do, then walk away. They aren't worth being around if they're gonna do that.

If you are scared of them, then make excuses. Tell them anything that will get you out of the situation. If you feel you can, though, it is a good idea to stand up to them—to let them know that they can't push you around.

—Janie, 14, England

WEBwatch

PEER TO PEER

Every girl and teen has sat through an assembly about the dangers of drug use. Usually the program is led by adults: police, doctors, teachers, or users. This article is about a different approach: peers. Going kid to kid, or teen to kid, is much more effective. Read about the program. Then talk to your school counselor about starting a peer counseling and prevention program.

http://www.mvonline.com/dhonline/dho0304-20.html

Q. Why do you think there is so much violence in the work-place today?

There's no right or wrong answer. Just circle what you think. Then look over your answers and talk about them with your friends.

1 People can't handle their emotions (when they are fired or put down at work).

Mostly disagree   Somewhat disagree   Somewhat agree   Mostly agree

2 People are afraid or unwilling to express their complaints to supervisors.

Mostly disagree   Somewhat disagree   Somewhat agree   Mostly agree

3 Violence is encouraged in the media.

Mostly disagree   Somewhat disagree   Somewhat agree   Mostly agree

4 Too many people are working below their ability level (getting frustrated).

Mostly disagree   Somewhat disagree   Somewhat agree   Mostly agree

5 Bosses are uncaring and rude to employees.

Mostly disagree   Somewhat disagree   Somewhat agree   Mostly agree

My Friends Smoke.
I Don't Want Them to Die!

The Problem I'm not sure what to say to my friends who smoke. I don't want to butt in, but I don't want them to die.

—Unsure

A Solution Dear Unsure: My best friend used to smoke too, but she stopped a while ago. I convinced her to stop smoking because why ruin your life at age 12 (my age). Even if your best friend isn't addicted, she could get addicted if she started smoking again.

You shouldn't start smoking even if it's "in" at your school and everyone else does. Smoking could be very dangerous. You should tell your friend the truth. Even if she laughs at it, tell her she should stop smoking because it's dangerous and you are afraid she'll die. If that doesn't work, tell a counselor at your school or tell your parent,s and they'll advise you on what to do. Tell someone if you care about your friend—even if you swore not to tell anyone!

STOP SMOKING

Want your parents or someone you know to stop smoking? Help them "Kick the Habit"? If you know someone who wants to quit, is thinking about it but needs help starting, this free Web site has lots of advice and tools to help them quit smoking.

http://www.quitnet.org
/qn_main.jtml

If you have more friends who don't smoke, then tell them and ask them what to do. Tell a big brother or sister (if you have one). They'll know what to do. We all have a part of our lives where everybody's smoking, drinking, or doing drugs. Call a teen hotline. There are special hotlines for these things, and you can talk to them and ask for advice. Remember! If you really care about your friend, tell SOMEONE!!!

—Stephanie, 12, Israel

I Want to Switch Schools!

The Problem I have been very stressed out with school lately. You see, I go to a very hard private school, and I really don't like any of my teachers and classes. I really want to change schools, but I know my parents (who have so much planned for their little girl) would be very upset if I asked them if I can switch schools. I want to please my parents, but I want to please myself at the same time! What should I do?

—Jane, 13, Tennessee

PROBLEMS AT SCHOOL?

Having problems keeping up with homework? Feel totally stressed at school? Check out this page. It can start you and your parents talking about how to help you cope.

http://msuinfo.ur.msstate.edu /~dur/nycu/nycukid.htm

A Solution Hey Jane! Well, first of all, no school is easy. They are all tough. I go to a public high school. Just a couple of months ago I was so busy at school that when I was at home, I literally had to pinch myself to make sure I was at home. I am not joking either. After a while, you will get straightened out at school, like I did.

If you really want to change schools, go ahead and tell your parents. They should understand. You need to understand your parents too. They just want you to be something wonderful later on in your life. First, see if there isn't something to like about your school. If not, talk to your parents about how you feel and why.

—Casey, 14, Tennessee

I Like a Guy Who's Bad for Me.

The Problem I like this boy who does drugs and has like 50,000 other girlfriends. He asked me out on a date, and I went out with him. He's asking me to do stuff I'm not ready to do. I don't know what to say to him. So I haven't said anything. What should I do about this problem?

—Ashley, 13

A Solution Dear Ashley: Don't let that guy turn you into another victim! If he is really faithful, he would give up all other girls to be with just you. I know, he'll tell you, "You're the only one for me. I'll be faithful." (He says this after the fifth time you've caught him cheating.) Who knows? The boy could change, but don't bet on it.

I have seen too many of my friends hurt by guys like these. These guys are empty. They don't really care for anyone. He'll try to make you a devoted girl while he goes and sees every other girl. Then the time will come where he does the, "It's just

Q. I caught my best friend taking some money out of my wallet! When she saw me, she apologized and acted as if nothing had happened. Now she is ignoring me. In school I have heard from other girls that she stole in shops or from them. What would you do if it happened to you?

There's no right or wrong answer. Just circle what you think. Then look over your answers and talk about them with your friends.

1 I'd tell my parents. Ask them to talk to her parents about it.

Mostly disagree   Somewhat disagree   Somewhat agree   Mostly agree

2 I'd get together with some of the other girls who have seen her steal and confront her to convince her to get counseling.

Mostly disagree   Somewhat disagree   Somewhat agree   Mostly agree

3 This is a serious problem. I'd tell the girl's parents so she can get help!

Mostly disagree   Somewhat disagree   Somewhat agree   Mostly agree

4 I'd tell everyone at school to watch their backs when she is around.

Mostly disagree   Somewhat disagree   Somewhat agree   Mostly agree

5 I'd ignore it and just make sure you aren't around when she steals.

Mostly disagree   Somewhat disagree   Somewhat agree   Mostly agree

not working out," or another popular one, "It's not you; it's me." Then, you'll be depressed when you should have known it was coming.

If he's trying to make you go too far, you've gotta say NO! It is your body. Don't let him do this to you. I have seen two of my best friends get pregnant because an older guy pressured them and they didn't say no. I've told guys no, and you can too. It's pretty simple! Please take my advice. I know all too well what might happen!

These are the steps I would take:

Tell him a simple, flat out NO!

If he continues to pressure you, walk away.

Tell someone.

NEVER EVER GIVE IN!

Hang out with girl buds till you trust the male race again. Once you do, do a background check on him. Ask around. Does he do drugs, drink, smoke, commit crimes, have past girlfriends he's pressured? Find it out!

Remember, it's your life and your body. I can't help you further than my keyboard, so it's up to you now.

—Amanda, 13, Michigan

Other Voices

A Solution   You really shouldn't be hanging out with this boy. Wait until he shapes up or, better yet, help him shape up! He isn't

In spite of everything, I still believe that people are really good at heart.

—Anne Frank
Submitted by
Kassadra, 11, Arkansas

When a Friend Shoplifts

Know a friend who shoplifts? Now THAT's trouble, right? Ever wonder why she does it? She's got money, so that's not it. Her parents buy her everything, so she's not deprived.

What does shoplifting do for her? Maybe it makes her feel powerful. Sneaky. Maybe she likes the danger, the heart-pounding thought that she might get caught. It's like a thrill ride, only free. You don't have to pay for the whole amusement park.

So what do YOU get when you keep _____ and when your friend keeps on _____?

Decide together if what you're doing is worth the price you're paying (for example: parents screaming, your future lost). Write down all the consequences you might face.

Want to make a change? Vow to help each other be your best selves. You go, girl! Get busy!

going to stop all of a sudden. But with your help, he might just squeeze through!

—Rose

A Solution

Ashley: You may really like him, but it sounds like this is a "love 'em and lose 'em" kinda guy. If he's really wrapped up in drugs, he's the kinda of guy you really need to steer clear of. Chances are if he's doing drugs, he's gonna pressure you to get into something you really don't want to do. You know that drugs kill people! If you really love this guy, though, try breaking his habits instead of giving him up. You do what's best. You know deep down what's right!

—Anna,11

Guys Are Seriously Fighting, and It's My Fault!

The Problem

I am 13, and I hang out with 17-year-old boys. When my mom found out, she grounded me for a month. When my brother's best friends found out, they said if they ever see the boys, they were going to hurt them real bad. A couple of days later, the boys were driving down the street and my brother's best

RACISM

Take a stand against racism! Join the YWCA in their "Stop Racism" Youth Campaign!

http://www.ywca.org/html /B4d17.asp

Q. The ENTIRE world should get off its backside and do something about all the violence, racism, pollution, and every other problem. What do you think?

— Polly, 13, Australia

There's no right or wrong answer. Just circle what you think. Then look over your answers and talk about them with your friends.

1 I say why should we? We won't be here to see the benefits.

Mostly disagree   Somewhat disagree   Somewhat agree   Mostly agree

2 I say definitely, not only for our sake but also the next generation's.

Mostly disagree   Somewhat disagree   Somewhat agree   Mostly agree

3 I think we should do a little to help our planet, but let's not get extreme.

Mostly disagree   Somewhat disagree   Somewhat agree   Mostly agree

4 I say our world isn't that bad. Can't we just ignore it for a little while longer?

Mostly disagree   Somewhat disagree   Somewhat agree   Mostly agree

5 I say get started. Let's set a good example for everyone else.

Mostly disagree   Somewhat disagree   Somewhat agree   Mostly agree

friend stopped them. They got into a fight and one of the boys hit my brother's best friend in the head with a baseball bat. He went to the hospital, and when my brother found out he said all of this was my fault. Is it?

—Anonymous, 13, USA

A Solution Hey Anonymous! You wrote a question because you wanted to know the truth. Well, I am not trying to be rude, awful, or just plain mean. I am going to tell you the truth.

First of all, a girl your age or my age has no right hanging out with 17-year-old boys. You are just asking for trouble. It would have been much safer if you had a mixture of ages from 12 years of age to 17 years of age to hang out with. Was this all your fault? In some ways, it was. Your mom had grounded you for seeing the boys and your brother's friends probably knew this. The boys were too old for you so you were just asking for trouble.

On the other hand, it was also your brother's friend's fault even though he wanted to protect you. Fighting and violence never solves anything, and it was not cool for him to get in a fight with this kid. Next time you see your brother's friend, tell him how much you appreciate what he did

WORLD AGAINST RACISM MEMORIAL

Check out the "World Against Racism Memorial" online museum. This is an exhibit that talks about the fiction of the idea of "race." It talks about the ignorance behind racism and the need to relate to all people as unique individuals rather than as members of a racial category. The memorial shows scenes of the experience of racism and how it destroys.

http://www.endracism.org/

Journalize It!

Everyone Says . . .

Ever hear your friends say, "But everyone says
_____ (fill in the blank)." For example:
Everyone says girls hate working on cars. Everyone
says grownups don't like movies like *Star Wars*.

The problem with this "but everyone says" sort of
thinking is that it can stop a good relationship in its
tracks. Say you want to talk to a guy. Before you even
meet him, you assume that he only wants to talk
"sports," even though he's not into that. Because of
that idea, you may never speak to him. Both of you
lose out. Thinking what "everyone says" about someone is prejudice, which is not cool.

Write down a time or two when someone close to you
said, "But everyone says . . ."

How does this kind of thinking affect your life?

Make a change. Decide to keep an eye on this sort of
thinking for the next week. You go, girl! Get busy!

for you. It will make him feel really good. Also tell him that you don't want any fighting in the future because of you. Try thinking things over. You should know whether the things you do are right or wrong. You need to hang out with kids your own age and always listen to your parents. They know what they are talking about.

—Casey, 14, Tennessee

STOP SCHOOL VIOLENCE!

This Web site helps you recognize the warning signs that may accompany violent behavior and what to do if you see it happen to someone you know.

http://www.ncpc.org/2schvio.htm

Hateful Minds

Last night I dreamed of gunshots,
they were ringing in my ears,
they hit lots of kids in their heads,
they brought many people tears.

They came from a gang's hateful minds,
they scared some teens half to death,
they frightened different teachers,
they shocked people, some called Beth.

In the developed countries there is a poverty of intimacy, a poverty of spirit, of loneliness, of lack of love. There is no greater sickness in the world today than that one.

—Mother Teresa
Submitted by
Elizabeth, 11, Nevada

Q. I think my friend's boyfriend is hitting her, but she claims she's just clumsy. What would you do if this happened to your friend?

— Erin, 15, Scotland

There's no right or wrong answer. Just circle what you think. Then look over your answers and talk about them with your friends.

1 This is serious. I'd try to convince her to tell her parents.

Mostly disagree   Somewhat disagree   Somewhat agree   Mostly agree

2 I'd get friends together and secretly watch my friend and her guy. Maybe we could catch him hitting her and get everyone to confront him.

Mostly disagree   Somewhat disagree   Somewhat agree   Mostly agree

3 I'd ask my friend to talk to a counselor at school or church.

Mostly disagree   Somewhat disagree   Somewhat agree   Mostly agree

4 If girls let their boyfriends hit them, they usually have low self-esteem. I'd try to help my friend build up her self-esteem.

Mostly disagree   Somewhat disagree   Somewhat agree   Mostly agree

5 I'd tell my friend that if she doesn't tell her parents she's being hurt, I will.

Mostly disagree   Somewhat disagree   Somewhat agree   Mostly agree

The Trench Coat Mafia did
    it all,
they gave the bullets to the
    dead,
they pained so many, large
    and tall,
they pumped them full of lead.

There were gunshots,
    gunshots, gunshots,
for as far as one could hear.
And when I woke this
    morning,
my face was wet with tears.

(This format is based on a
poem by Gary Pulsen.)

—Written by
Johanna, 12, Illinois
Edited by Nicole, 14, Ohio

You Can Quote Me on That

The mind is not (typed by gender).

—Margaret Mead
Submitted by
Courtney, 12, Mississippi

WEB watch

SWEATSHOP CONDITIONS

Where do you find out about manufacturers whose clothing or goods are created under sweatshop conditions (women and children working long hours for little pay)? Here's one coalition of students, labor, and community groups who want to make the dollars they spend count.

http://www.sweatshopwatch
.org/

Q. What do you think we should do about the guns in our schools?

—Bridget, 10, USA

There's no right or wrong answer. Just circle what you think. Then look over your answers and talk about them with your friends.

1 I think we should put metal detectors in all schools.

Mostly disagree   Somewhat disagree   Somewhat agree   Mostly agree

2 I think we should place hall monitors to make sure no one has a gun.

Mostly disagree   Somewhat disagree   Somewhat agree   Mostly agree

3 I think we should have locker searches.

Mostly disagree   Somewhat disagree   Somewhat agree   Mostly agree

4 I think we should have stricter consequences for kids who bring guns to school.

Mostly disagree   Somewhat disagree   Somewhat agree   Mostly agree

5 I think we should have an award program for people who turn guns in.

Mostly disagree   Somewhat disagree   Somewhat agree   Mostly agree

Q. I'm having trouble with a teacher. She seems to only talk to me when I'm getting into trouble. But yet she says she wants to have a close "mother-daughter" relationship with me. How can I have that relationship if all she does is chew me out? She is really confusing me! What would you do if this was happening to you?

—Hannah, 14, Missouri

There's no right or wrong answer. Just circle what you think. Then look over your answers and talk about them with your friends.

1 I'd just confront her. I'd tell her I want to be friendly, but she's got to stop chewing me out.

Mostly disagree   Somewhat disagree   Somewhat agree   Mostly agree

2 I'd have to think about it. Why am I getting in trouble? Can I change my behavior so she won't have to get mad at me?

Mostly disagree   Somewhat disagree   Somewhat agree   Mostly agree

3 Teachers shouldn't be like mothers. It's not her job to be my mom or chew me out. That's why I'd tell my parents what she said.

Mostly disagree   Somewhat disagree   Somewhat agree   Mostly agree

4 I'd tell the principal or a counselor that I want to be moved to another class.

Mostly disagree   Somewhat disagree   Somewhat agree   Mostly agree

5 I'd just ignore her. I won't be in her class forever.

Mostly disagree   Somewhat disagree   Somewhat agree   Mostly agree

Dealing with Depression and Death

They Call Me "Moody," But I'm Terribly Depressed!

The Problem I don't know what is wrong with me. A couple of times I have thought of committing suicide because I thought life was unbearable. I didn't tell anyone because I feel as if no one cares. It seems as if nobody has time for that pesky kid who always has one of her moods. That pesky kid is me.

Although I'm better now, I still am in that depressed mood. I am afraid that sooner or later something will drive me over the edge. I feel as if my family has deserted me. I am willing to restore the old me in which I had a profound respect for life, but I don't know how. Any suggestions?

—Jeana, 12, Japan

A Solution

Hey Jeana! Your feelings aren't unusual. Many teens think of suicide. The best thing to do, even if you think no one cares, is to tell someone. Your mom, sister, brother, dad, or best friend are all people that I am sure REALLY care about you and will love to help you. If they learn from you that you aren't just in a "mood" or being "pesky" but seriously feel that life sometimes isn't worth living and you need help, they'll make time for you.

You might have a chemical imbalance that a doctor could help. I'm sure there are teen crisis hotlines in Japan that you can call. There are many Web sites to help teens in crisis if you aren't quite ready to talk to adults yet.

Even at A Girl's World, a pen pal will gladly listen, I am sure. When you get into that depressed mood, you can talk or just type it out till you feel you are better and feel more like your "old" self again.

—Jen, 14, Washington

How wonderful to be happy for no reason.

—Greta Garbo
Submitted by
Renee, 10, Canada

STRESS

What is stress? What causes it? How can you deal with it? This site has a free book on stress management. It includes lots of ways to deal with student stresses, like boyfriend problems and trouble at school. Check it out!

http://www.teachhealth.com/

Editor's Note: Also, physical activity can help depression "lift." When you feel that way, put on a fav CD and jump around, ride your bike, or jog. Physical activity produces chemicals in the brain that counter depression!

I'm Constantly Overwhelmed with Everything!

The Problem I'm overwhelmed! Total stress! I've got too much homework, my parents are always on my back. There are never enough hours in the day! Nothing is fun anymore. Help!

—Dina, 15

A Solution Hey Dina! Let's face it, we have all experienced stress before, whether it be doing a piece of homework at the last minute or your mum nagging you about your untidy bedroom. The way to deal with stress is plan your time. If you have a nine-page essay that you have two weeks to do, do a page a day instead of rushing it the night before. Give yourself rewards. Every hour you do of homework, put a quarter in a jar, then treat yourself at the end of the week! Don't do all your homework in one go. Have a 5-minute rest every 40 minutes, and make yourself a cup of tea!

If stress is really bothering you, talk to a sympathetic adult, a parent, aunt, or teacher, for example. They may have suggestions on how to cope with stress and the best way to deal with it. Take up a worthwhile hobby, such as learning an instrument or dancing. This gives you something different to do and something to look forward to. If life becomes too hard to cope

Q. What would you do if you were totally s-t-r-e-s-s-e-d-o-u-t?

—Kristie, 15, Wisconsin

There's no right or wrong answer. Just circle what you think. Then look over your answers and talk about them with your friends.

1 I'd plan some "down time" to just think.

Mostly disagree   Somewhat disagree   Somewhat agree   Mostly agree

2 I'd blow off at least some activities. You can't do everything.

Mostly disagree   Somewhat disagree   Somewhat agree   Mostly agree

3 I'd ask my parents to help me deal.

Mostly disagree   Somewhat disagree   Somewhat agree   Mostly agree

4 I'd form a "stress-busters" club with friends and talk about what's bugging me.

Mostly disagree   Somewhat disagree   Somewhat agree   Mostly agree

5 I'd ask teachers to help.

Mostly disagree   Somewhat disagree   Somewhat agree   Mostly agree

with, chill out with your friends! Go to the movies, go out for a day! Try to keep calm and manage your time well. That's my advice. Have a nice life!

—Alice, 14, England

Editor's note: If you can cut down on some of the groups or clubs that demand your time, you might have to make that decision. Get a planner book and write down a schedule that you can live with. Decide what you just can't fit in any longer and let it go for now.

**Dark Enraptures:
Poetry of Pain**

*A world of darkness,
A world in pain;
A childhood forgotten,
Tucked sadly away.
A new life started,
Yet with nowhere to hide,*

*From the pain gnawing me
On the inside.
I crave to remember,
My past shaded black,
And yet I am scared,
To let the memories
Come back.*

—Written by
Rachael, 12, Australia
Edited by
Melody, 13, California

SUICIDE PREVENTION

Contact a group like the American Foundation for Suicide Prevention. There's great information on suicide prevention, teen and youth suicide, and dealing with depression.

http://www.afsp.org
/index-1.htm

My Best Friend Talks About Death a Lot.

The Problem My best friend is 15 and she's really depressed. She broke up with her boyfriend, and now she thinks her whole life is over. Lately, she's been joking about killing herself. And she talks about death a lot. No one else thinks she's serious. Everybody says she's just trying to get attention. I don't know. I'm scared something will happen. What do I do? Please help me!

—Deborah, 15

DEALING WITH DEATH

Dealing with death isn't easy for anyone. Here's an article about how teens deal with death that can help. There are links on the page to kids and death and dealing with the loss of a pet. We hope this helps!

http://www.dying.about.com /health/dying/library/weekly /aa102697.htm

A Solution Hey Deborah! Your best friend is soooo lucky to have you in her life. You've got your eyes open. Three of the big, big warning signs about suicide for teens are feeling depressed or down or hopeless, talking or joking about killing yourself, and talking about death. You see what's going on. Your friend needs somebody to talk to sooo bad. Keep her talking to you! Ask her why she feels this way. Tell her you love her.

This part's hard, but you've got to get her in touch with help and fast. That means a school counselor or a grownup you both trust or her family. Don't be foolin' around thinking you can talk her out of this thing. You can't. It's not your job. Get on the phone and call a suicide hotline or a crisis hotline in your town, fast! There's a book called *Survivors of Suicide* by Rita Robinson that's really good. She writes about what can help and what you can do. Check it out. I hope this helps!

—Rachel, 14, Washington

Someone Who Inspired Me

I've had many stars in my life, but none shone brighter than my friend Ms. J. When she came to live on this island with her family, she brought with her the true meaning of life. During her two years here, she taught me how to care for others. She brought me closer to God than I ever thought possible. I was able to tell her anything and know that she would pray with me and ask for His guidance and support. She taught me to share and care. She taught me to love when I would rather hate. She opened up a whole new world to me. She was a true friend, a friend I wished would be around forever.

She sensed my need for friends and involved me with the Corp Cadets youth program. One Friday before a Girl Guard (another youth

"You Can **Quote** Me on That"

I wanted a perfect ending. Now I've learned, the hard way, that some poems don't rhyme. Some stories don't have a clear beginning, middle, or end. Life is about not knowing and having to change. It's about taking the moment and making the best of it, without knowing what's going to happen next.

—Gilda Radner
Submitted by
Angel, 13, Oregon

Q. If you ever felt so depressed or knew someone that was so depressed they felt suicidal, what would you do? What should you do if you or a friend has suicidal thoughts or feelings?

There's no right or wrong answer. Just circle what you think. Then look over your answers and talk about them with your friends.

1 I'd tell them, "Don't think you're weird or nuts. Everyone gets depressed. It's time to get help."

Mostly disagree   Somewhat disagree   Somewhat agree   Mostly agree

2 Call someone and talk. Look at the phone book for a crisis or suicide prevention line. Get a close friend on the line.

Mostly disagree   Somewhat disagree   Somewhat agree   Mostly agree

3 I'd say they should tell someone what they are thinking and feeling. Don't hide anything.

Mostly disagree   Somewhat disagree   Somewhat agree   Mostly agree

4 I'd get out and away. Do something else. Go be with a friend. Do something active. Sometimes this can get you out of a suicidal depression.

Mostly disagree   Somewhat disagree   Somewhat agree   Mostly agree

5 I'd tell them to seek help immediately. Don't think this will go away or get better. Talk to a clergy person, school counselor, someone you can trust who will take you seriously.

Mostly disagree   Somewhat disagree   Somewhat agree   Mostly agree

group I am in) meeting, Ms. J asked me to come into her office. She gave me a journal. She knew that I liked to write, and she told me to use the journal to write out my feelings. Two days later I was told she had died. No one knows how, and no one knows why.

I think it's just that God called her home. Even though I wish it wasn't true, I still have to live with the fact that Lieutenant J was gone. People had me say "good-bye" to her, but I know I don't have to because I'll see my friend again in heaven, and friends don't say good-bye.

—Kathie, 12, Micronesia

When I Get Angry, I Cut Myself. Help Me!

The Problem I am having a lot of problems with friends, so I started cutting my arm. I know this is wrong. What else can I do to release my anger?

—Lucy, 14, Missouri

A Solution Hey Lucy! I think you should tell your friends how you feel instead of cutting your arm from anger. Let them know what is bothering you and see if you can work it out. If they don't care or won't change and it is still making you feel angry, I'd say you don't need to be around them. Maybe you should talk to your parent(s) or an adult about the way you cut your arm when you are angry.

—Carri, 15, Indiana

Q. My dad just died about three weekends ago, and I am scared to live without him. What can I do? What would you do if it happened to you?

—Sam, 9

There's no right or wrong answer. Just circle what you think. Then look over your answers and talk about them with your friends.

1 I'd try to realize that he'll always be there in my memory. I'd make a scrapbook of pictures, family mementos of fun times with Dad.

Mostly disagree   Somewhat disagree   Somewhat agree   Mostly agree

2 I'd get counseling from an adult at church or school.

Mostly disagree   Somewhat disagree   Somewhat agree   Mostly agree

3 I'd tell my other family members how I felt and talk it out together.

Mostly disagree   Somewhat disagree   Somewhat agree   Mostly agree

4 I'd talk to other kids who have recently lost one or both of their parents.

Mostly disagree   Somewhat disagree   Somewhat agree   Mostly agree

Editor's Note: Lucy, you must take this problem seriously. If anger or depression is what drives you to cut yourself, then, in addition to Carri's good advice, try anger-releasing activities like putting on a great CD and dancing wildly, playing any sport, something physical and healthy (punch that punching bag) to release the anger. For more tips, call 1-800-DONT-CUT or find *Skin Game: A Cutter's Memoir* by Caroline Kettlewell or *Cutting: Understanding and Overcoming Self-Mutilation* by Steven Leverkron at your local library or bookstore.

Seventeen magazine did an article on the subject in their June 1996 issue (also available at the library). If you keep razor blades or other sharp objects in your purse, room, or backpack, get rid of them!!! Also, check the net search engines (like Ask Jeeves) under self-mutilation for Web sites that can help. You aren't alone!

He Went Back to His Ex. I Just Want to Die!

The Problem   I have been having a lot of problems. I just lost a guy I am truly in love with because he still loves his ex-girlfriend. I can't stand this. I love him so much. I just want to die—maybe that's the answer. I should just end it all. I don't think I can live without him; it hurts too much. What should I do?

—"Suicide," 16

A Solution   Hey "Suicide!" It may seem harsh, but you do seem to be overreacting a little. I know it hurts now, but there are

WEB watch

SUICIDE

Have questions about suicide? Can anything be done for someone who is that depressed? Check out this wonderful site by the family of Jared Benjamin High, who died at 13 from severe depression. Jared's family pay tribute to their son and talk about the true cost of suicide.

Their question and answer page is incredible.

http://www.jaredstory.com/

very few relationships that start at 16 and go on forever, and it is likely that you will have many more boyfriends before you find someone to stay with permanently.

Try to respect him for his decision to break it off. It must have taken a lot of courage to admit to you that he was still in love with someone else, and stringing you along would have been so much worse. Be glad you found out the truth! Now you can find someone who isn't carrying a torch for his ex!

—Janie, 14, England

When My Stepmom Died, I Lost My Confidence!

The Problem I recently lost my stepmom to cancer. This has been very hard on me. I previously lost my actual mom to AIDS when I was 4. I'm afraid no one cares about me anymore, and I have become very shy and not as outgoing as I once was.

Please help me try to regain my once confident, assured self.

—Katie, 14, Minnesota

A Solution   Hey Katie! People do care about you, not just family, but your friends too. You have the right to grieve over your stepmom. You need to get back to your regular schedule. Start with small steps. Go to your friend's house after school. I too have lost a family member a long time ago. At first it was very hard not seeing him every day after school. Eventually I realized that I would have to deal with his death.

I coped with his death by being around family and remembering the good times. Slowly your joy of life will come back. Remember that your stepmom probably wouldn't want you to withdraw from your life but keep on going as you were or better! I hope that you feel better about yourself. Here is a Web site for grieving: http://www.grieving.org

—Suzanne, 13, Florida

Since Our Cat Died, Nothing Is the Same!

The Problem   About a week ago, my cat died. It was like a family member, and now everyone in my family is upset. Now nothing is the same. What should I do?

—Patti, 12, Michigan

A Solution   Hey Patti! It is always very upsetting to lose a loved one. I'm very sorry to hear this about your cat, but after every loss there is a time of grieving for that person or creature. It is not best to try and forget your cat because it sounds as if it had a very important role to play in your life. Instead, try to remember the cat by hanging up pictures on your wall or making a scrapbook of your cat's things and pictures of it. I have a friend who has a little memorial place in her bedroom where she keeps her photos of her deceased animals.

If looking at the pictures right now makes you even more depressed, it might help to talk things over with your family and close friends to let them know how you feel about this. Share fun memories of great times with your cat, funny things he or she did, what a good life your pet had, etc. There is a good chance that your loved ones will understand, and when you feel really low, you can always have a good chat with them. Try not to be too upset about this, and try to cheer up your family a bit too (if you can).

Good Luck!

—Callan, 12, England

The Silky Cat

A silky cat got up from beneath the trees,
And licked his fur with a cold blowing breeze,
He stretched his claws and called out to a friend,
They chased each other around the highway's bend.

A car came speeding around the corner,
The cat's friend screamed and jumped over the border.
The silky cat was all alone,
And walked on crying a sad soft moan.

The cat's hair bristled in the soft night's air,
She went onto the street where there was a fair.
She walked past a mother and daughter, an ice cream they shared.
She walked through a blizzard of people, none of whom cared.

The silky cat seemed to
  wander the earth,
In search for a friend
She walked to Perth,
A hole in her heart which she
  needed to mend.

The cat walked until she was
  found,
Unfortunately, by a pound.
They held a needle like a
  portal,
She meowed and became
  Immortal.

A silky cat once got up from
  beneath a tree,
And let her soul fly with a
  breeze.
She stretched her claws and
  called to her friend,
A heart that didn't need a
  mend
As they chased each other
  around the highway's
  bend.

GRIEF AND GRIEVING

Here's a Web site that's all about dealing with grief and grieving. When someone you love dies, your feelings of sadness can become overwhelming. When a pet dies, it can be really hard because you feel like there's no one to go to. That's where "Ask Kitty" comes to the rescue. She's a trained psychotherapist whose specialty is grief and loss. You can find her at:

http://www.death-dying.com
/petloss.htm

Another wonderful Web site is:
http://www.petloss.com/

—Written by Catherine, 13, Australia
Edited by Anna, 11, New York

Someone I Look Up To

My brightest star is my dad. He's my hero. My dad has been raising me and my older sister alone since my mom died five years ago. He's the greatest. He is always there for me, and I would just like to thank him. I love you, Daddy.

—Kelsey, 9, Illinois

Q. I just got over losing one of my best friends to AIDS. He was my age and I'd always had a major crush on him. I'm hurting and my friends try to help, but for some reason I just back away from them. What would you do if this was happening to you?

—"Lucky Diamond," 15, California

There's no right or wrong answer. Just circle what you think. Then look over your answers and talk about them with your friends.

1 There are support groups everywhere for people whose friends have died of AIDS. I'd ask my school counselor to find one for me. Sometimes it's easier to talk to strangers than to friends.

Mostly disagree   Somewhat disagree   Somewhat agree   Mostly agree

2 I'd explain to my friends that I appreciate their support but just am not ready to talk right now.

Mostly disagree   Somewhat disagree   Somewhat agree   Mostly agree

3 If the boy had any family members I knew really well, I'd go to them and, together, find a support group.

Mostly disagree   Somewhat disagree   Somewhat agree   Mostly agree

4 If I had a crush on him and never told him, I'd try going to his grave and "talking" to him or write him a letter. I'd tell him how I felt and let him go. I think doing this would help me move on.

Mostly disagree   Somewhat disagree   Somewhat agree   Mostly agree

5 I'd go to the local hospital or hospice and volunteer to help other kids with AIDS. In a way, I think I'd feel like I was helping my friend.

Mostly disagree   Somewhat disagree   Somewhat agree   Mostly agree

My Friend Is Dying! What Do I Do?

I have this friend at church who has a brain tumor. The tumor is down by the roots of her brain, and if the doctors did a surgery there, she'd be sure to die. She's gonna have the doctors do something else to her head to try to make the tumor go away, and my mom says that she'll probably die. HELP! She's my only friend who didn't ever turn her back on me! And all my other friends are being mean to me! If she dies, how do I deal with it? What do I do to make nice friends?

—Joy, 11, Indiana

A Solution Hey Joy! This is one serious problem, and you can't keep her from dying. Anyway, she might not die, and she might get through the operation. My neighbor had the same problem and he got tough with it; now he's fine. And your mother might be wrong too. Even the doctors don't know exactly what her chances are, and she might have more chances of surviving than dying.

HELPING A FRIEND WHO IS DYING

This Web site has important ideas about what to do, how and when to act, and what to say, when a friend is dying.

http://www.hospicenet.org /html/help_a_friend.html

As for your friends, you have to choose them. Try chatting with people in your class, church, or out-of-school activities that you don't always relate with. They might end up being nicer than your current friends. Now is a time for you to be surrounded by good, caring pals—not "friends" who are "mean" to you. Your current friends don't sound like friends to me!

—María, 12, Spain

Someone I Look Up To

My teacher, Mrs. H, taught me everything I needed to know. A while back a friend from school was hit by a car and killed. My teacher knew we had been close friends. When I walked into school, one of my friends told me in the hall and I burst into tears. I ran into the nearest room, which just happened to be my friend Jake's homeroom teacher's (my friend who was hit by the car), and he was also crying. He took me into his arms and called for my teacher. She came in and let me and a couple of my friends go into another room. We sat and sobbed until she came in and comforted us, telling us that we have the right to be angry and sad. When I got to the funeral, I saw Mrs. H there, and she sat me down and we had a long talk. She was the one that pulled me through those hard times. Thank you, Mrs. H!

—Sara, 12, USA

My Boyfriend Died in a Car Crash!

The Problem One of my best friends and my boyfriend died in a car accident. I had just visited him that morning. Once my father told me about him, I burst out crying. Can you please help me deal with the loss of my boyfriend?

—Erin, 18, USA

A Solution Hey Erin! I am really sorry to hear of your bad news. I cannot take the pain away, but here are a few suggestions to help ease it a bit and to help you feel a little bit better.

This may be very hard, but visiting the graves and saying good-bye officially can help a lot. Wait until you feel you are ready or this could just upset you even more. But if you feel that you can face this, it could be very helpful for you. You can visit the grave, have a little (or major) cry (it does help you feel a bit better), say good-bye properly, and leave them some flowers, or something special to you, as a sign of your love and respect.

If there is anything you wish you had said to your boyfriend or best friend, or anything you would like to say now, you could write it all down in a letter and get it off your chest. Writing a letter and telling your friends how you feel might make you feel better.

Although you want to remember your friends, and you probably have lots of treasured photos of them, keeping photos of them on view all over your room will probably only upset you and make you feel worse, as you will be reminded of them everywhere you look. So how about making a memory drawer? Fill it with all your photos of them and all your treasured possessions that remind you of them, and then you can look in it whenever you want and be reminded of happy times with them.

Why not find an E-pal to talk to about this? You can use A Girl's World's pen pal function to find a pen pal who is dealing with a death at the moment.

If you want to talk to a professional instead, phone childline for free (it does NOT show up on your phone bill!) or visit their Web site at http://www.teleschool.org.ukchildline. When it gets late at night, it is easy to just lie in bed and think about sad things that have happened for hours. Try and think about something else, or read a book or magazine and put it out of your mind.

Remember that your friends and family are there to support you. Don't shut them out! Tell them how you feel and ask for advice, or just talk and laugh over things that you have done in the past with your other friend and boyfriend and happy times you have all spent together. Also, don't spend all your time dwelling on this sad event.

Concentrate on you! Let your friends support you by taking your mind off everything; go out and have fun with them! You may find at times that you find yourself laughing and having fun, and then you suddenly remember your friends and feel guilty. Don't! You are allowed to be happy. It doesn't mean you do not love your friend and your boyfriend; it just means that you are coping well. You deserve to be happy. You will never forget your friend and boyfriend, but as time goes on, the pain will lessen. I promise you!

—Shannon, 15, England

A Solution

Recently I lost one of my brothers in a horrifying car accident. Although it happened a month ago I wanted to share this poem with you.

COMPASSIONATE FRIENDS

Lost a brother or a sister? Family looking for support? The Compassionate Friends are a nonprofit Web site devoted to helping people deal with the loss of a child.

http://www.compassionate friends.org/

God Took One Away

I had two wonderful brothers,
God took one away,
Now I live in sorrow,
While in heaven he will
Stay.

I had two wonderful brothers,
But as you can see,
No matter where he is
He'll always be a brother to me.

—Written by
Sara, 14, Wisconsin
Edited by
Angela, 12, England

Forgive Me

One year ago,
My sister and I got into a fight.
A year ago I didn't know,
This fight would hurt me in the night.

She was going out on a date
And leaving me all alone.
She promised we would have some cake,
Instead, she chose some guy with cologne.

They went to a party with friends,
but they didn't make it home that night.
He drove down a road that led to their ends,
Without even a warning in sight.

He was driving while drunk
And now they're both dead.
You can't pack a trunk
To go where they did.

Please forgive me sister,
I never got to say I was sorry.

—Written by Rebecca, 15, Minnesota

Join the Fun!

Like the book? Check out the Web site! Come, join the fun!

What People Are Saying About Us

USA TODAY, **Featured as "Everything a Girl Could Want":**
"Since 1996, the only online magazine with daily, weekly, and monthly features written and edited by girls and teens."

Snipped from *The New York Times:*
"There are a few wonderful sites that present utterly absorbing, enjoyable and comparatively safe places for preteenage and teen-age girls. In fact, I'm convinced that, taken together, Web sites like the ones reviewed here—Girl Tech, Purple Moon, and A Girl's World—may just be the "killer app" for girls. . . . A Girl's World is run by a staff of volunteers, almost all of whom are girls

themselves. The result is an admirable, if unsophisti-
cated, ezine for girls (that is an) amazing testament to
the creative energy of its visitors. . . . Although the
presentation of A Girl's World is simple and straight-
forward—nearly everything is rendered in text—it has
a greater abundance of spirit than a Girl Scout cookout
. . . refreshing."

**Snipped from Spun Gold Award for Excellence from
Kid's Domain:**
"This is a wonderful site for girls, with great content.
Any girl who wants to can submit an article, and get
credit for it! They will also receive a free year's member-
ship to Gold Key Circle and the safety measures (in a
Gold Key) are exemplary. There is no advertising, no
hidden agenda, just girls having fun!

   "I simply can't praise this site enough! I couldn't find one
thing I didn't like about it, and I am pretty picky about
what I let my girls do and see. I have never been crazy
about the idea of kids chat rooms, either, but I like the
idea of the membership, password protected chat
rooms. . . . The articles are well-written and informative,
the crafts are fun, the teen advice column is right on target
with teen concerns, and being able to contribute your
own articles is a wonderful idea! A Girl's World Online
Club is definitely deserving of our Gold Award for Excellence."

Snipped from the *Los Angeles Times,* **reviewed by:
www.4kids.org:**
"A Girl's World Online Clubhouse is an incredible online
experience just for girls. As 'the space where girls rule the
place,' this monthly magazine is for girls of the 90s.
There is so much you could do, you could stay for days.
Make new friends, get to know women with dynamite

careers, find directions for neat stuff you can make and lots more! Girls are in the clubhouse, waiting for you to come share your thoughts on a million different subjects. So go, girl, and have a blast at the place 'where it's cool to be a girl!'"

What Girls Say About AGW

"This place rules!! I spend like 20 hours on here a month!"

—Jen

"I think it's awesome that people like you guys could start something like this. It's cool, and safe, just what on-line girlz need. KEEP UP THE GOOD WORK!"

—Shelley

"The Penpal program is great! And I LOVE the Baby-sitting classes! That's why it's a big thing 4 me. (The teacher's) doing a GREAT job! GIRLS' WORLD RULES!! Love,"

—Melissa

"I think the club is great. I pop in to the page every day when I get time."

—Aviva

"I got to talk to a real rocket scientist! I can't wait to tell all my friends. I love science. I want to be a scientist when I grow up."

—Holly

"This is one cool place for GIRLS where girls aren't expected to be wimps."

—Mallory

"When I first got here, I thought this would be all about makeup, prissy stuff like that. But it's not, so it's cool!"
—Samantha

"Hey! I just wanted to thank you for making this so fun. I am 15 and I am having lots of fun and was surprised to find people my age when I found this site. *THANKS ALOT!*"
—RDUDA

What Adults Say About AGW

"I recently had the pleasure of visiting AGW and was thrilled with what I found! It's such a pleasure to see a magazine for girls that doesn't dwell on "hot hunks" or how to increase your (physical) appeal. Girls of this age desperately need to be valued for who they are, not for how close they come to some Hollywood ideal . . . it's wonderful that you profile women of true achievement, not just models and actresses. Young girls need to have women to look up to, and you are doing a great job in providing role models."
—Kelly

"I very much believe in what you're doing for young girls. I think it's critical to have girl sites that don't just hawk the latest makeup trends, but that really promote independence and unique thinking. In any case, kudos to you for what you're doing. We need more young girls to have self-confidence."
—Heather I.

Awards

New members join every day, based on the recommendations of teachers, parents, and major search engines like Yahooligans, which rated us one of the "coolest" magazines for girls on the Web.

AGW was the first online site for girls recommended by CNN Interactive. Our Penpal Spectacular was cited by a major consumer reporting magazine. We've been awarded The Point's coveted "Top 5% of the Web" award and were cited as the best site for girls on the Web by the *San Diego Union Tribune*. We've been featured in other media, such as the *Los Angeles Times'* Cutting Edge, on KFI 640 am radio, and by *Family PC* magazine, along with numerous other awards.

We are recommended and listed by Sprint, Lycos, CNN, Prodigy Kids Pages, Cochran Kids Sites, Kidscom, About Me, 4Kids.org, Peekaboo, World Village, WWWomen.com, On Ramp-Canada, Femina, Whidbey-Australia. Altogether about 1,400 other sites have created links to A Girl's World Online Clubhouse.

Use the Gold Key Chat Club to Meet New Friends

Give and get advice, get a pen pal without publishing your e-mail address, and do what you love to do—chat, meet great guests, post on message boards, play games, take our online class, and take our Babysitter's Certificate Class—all for free! It's a cool deal, a whole year of chat! That's a $5.00 value— FREE for any girl who buys this book! So grab your parents and fill out this form to join the fun!

What Gold Key Is: Gold Key is a private, member-supported chat club just for girls and teens the world over, ages 7–17. For information about what this members-only chat club is all about, go here:

http://www.agirlsworld.com/clubgirl/gold-key/chatworks.html

Privacy and Information Use Policy: A Girl's World Online Clubhouse does not rent, sell, or give out e-mail addresses, addresses, mailing lists, or personally identifiable information about girls to anyone else. Ever. Period. All information on this form is kept strictly private and is used solely for signup, security, and contact information. We will not provide this information to any third party.

A Girl's World Gold Key Circle
Chat Club Membership Form

I, (Parent's Name) _____ certify that I am the parent or legal guardian of (Daughter's Name) _____, age _____.

I hereby give my permission for my daughter to participate in the Gold Key Circle Chat Club. By signing up for and using this chatservice, my daughter and I agree that we have read and agreed to follow these chat club rules at http://www.agirlsworld.com/clubgirl/gold-key/rules.html and Terms of Service at http://www.agirlsworld.com/clubgirl/gold-key/terms.html. I understand that AGW reserves the right to delete without warning or refund, any member of the Gold Key Circle Chat Club who violates the Chat Club rules or Terms of Service.

Signed:

(Parent's Signature) _____ Date _____

Passcode Contact Information: We'll send your daughter's Gold Key passcode by e-mail to the e-mail address below.

E-mail address _____

If we're unable to complete your daughter's chat club signup, our club will send a postcard to your mailing address. We will not provide this information to any third party.

Mailing address:

Street:_____ Apt./PO:_____

City: _____ State: _____ Zip Code: _____

Country (if not USA): _____

International Postal Code: _____

Finish Your Signup

- Parents, please tear out, fill out, and sign this form. No facsimiles, please.
- Don't forget to check to see that the e-mail address is filled out so we can complete your signup.
- Mail your completed form to:

A Girl's World Online Clubhouse
Attn: Prima Books: Free Chat Club/Pen Pals Offer
825 College Blvd. PBO 102-442
Oceanside, CA 92057

This signed permission form will complete your daughter's application. We will create a Gold Key Chat Club user name for her and mark her account as "paid" with full access for one year just as soon as this signed permission form is received. Thank you for helping us provide a safe, fun chat area for girls on the Web!

Problems? Get Help!

It can take up to a week after we receive your signed permission form to give your daughter access to the chat club. If you don't hear from us within 10 days, please do the following: First, send a message to lost-gk-pass@agirlsworld.com. The computer will let you know if we have a Gold Key user name for your daughter. If you get back an e-mail that says "no user name" and you sent in your form, please send an e-mail describing the problem to gk-problems@agirlsworld.com, and we will check it out.

Thanks again to Prima Publishing and their support in making this the place where girls and teens rule the Web!

Meet the Editor

My name is J. Christine Gardner. I'm 12 years old. I was born in Oceanside, California on August 18, 1988. I have 2 older brothers: Mike, 17, and Anthony, soon to be 15. My mom's name is Juanita and my dad is Blane. Some of my dreams for the future are to go to Stanford University and become a pediatric surgeon.

If I were to describe myself to someone I've never met before, I'd say that I'd rather be laughing than have a serious chat. And for fun I'd want to be playing outside with my best friend. When I feel blue, I just imagine that nobody is around and I listen to music.

The most challenging thing I've ever done was to learn how to walk again after a hip operation. The most exciting thing I've ever done was to fly an airplane by myself. (There was a real pilot in the passenger seat though).

My experiences being a part of the AGW girlcrew have been great. I've gone on fun field trips, and I've learned a lot. The club has changed a little bit since I joined three years ago. Now we have a lot more really cool activities and we've gotten more publicity too. And being a member of AGW is like being a mini-movie star. You get to be in the paper, on the Internet, and—the thing that I like best—you get a bunch of respect. Those are some of the things that keep me coming back every week. I also come back every week because the other girls in the crew are really nice, and since they don't go to my school, or live by me, that's the only chance I get to see them.

Being a member of AGW makes me feel like I'm wanted or that I'm needed somewhere. I really like to feel like I belong to someone or something. In fact, by being a member of AGW, I've changed in a way that my mom has wanted me to change for as long as I can remember. I've become more girlie.

For me, editing my first book was like I was a genius, because I always pictured authors as being the smartest in their classes and dominating their schools. And editing this book was really hard because I had to keep up with studying and my homework.

I have three role models: my oldest brother, Mike; my dad; and a sergeant in the Civil Air Patrol, Leslie Borenstein. They make me laugh, smile, and feel good about myself. The advice I have for other girls who want to be writers: Choose a tense, then structure it into well thought-out sentences. And the thing I like most about being a girl today is that girls are as equal as boys!

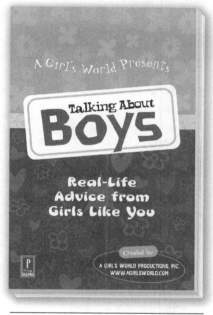

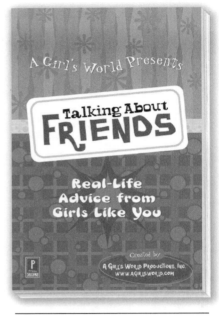